AN ITALIAN VINTAGE

Other books by Lynn M. Turner:

Adieu, My Love
Cutter's Wake
Growing Attraction

AN ITALIAN VINTAGE

•

Lynn M. Turner

1~10

AVALON BOOKS
NEW YORK

Published by Thomas Bouregy & Co., Inc.
160 Madison Avenue, New York, NY 10016

Library of Congress Cataloging-in-Publication Data

Turner, Lynn M.
  An Italian vintage / Lynn M. Turner.
     p. cm.
  ISBN 978-0-8034-9993-5
  1. Canadians—Italy—Fiction.   2. Vendetta—Fiction.
3. Italy—Fiction.   4. Domestic fiction.   I. Title.
  PR9199.3.T837I83 2010
  813'.54—dc22
                                             2009024247

PRINTED IN THE UNITED STATES OF AMERICA
ON ACID-FREE PAPER
BY HADDON CRAFTSMEN, BLOOMSBURG, PENNSYLVANIA

To Cindy T. Moss, who contributed more
to the writing of this book than she's willing to
admit, and to Bonita and Daniel Slunder, and
the wonderful people of Masseis, Italia.

Chapter One

The Italian sun warmed her shoulders as Libby jabbed the key at the hole in the little brass circle on the ancient door. It definitely did not fit. She turned it over and tried the other way. Again. With an exasperated groan, she swung around, paced across the cobbled patio, and sank onto a stone bench next to her pile of luggage. It felt like weeks, rather than one day, since she had boarded her plane in Toronto. Every fiber of her body ached with exhaustion.

She looked to the left and counted to be sure she was, in fact, three doors from the corner that led to the village square. The house facade looked almost as she remembered too: three stories, stone walls, evenly spaced, lofty-yet-narrow windows bracketed by dark green shutters, and an exterior staircase with a tall decorative iron gate at the bottom. The gate opened onto a cement footpath where the steps rose to a beautiful balcony on the third floor—assuming the balcony was still structurally sound.

What were her options? She supposed she could find her grandmother's sister, Erika Kidric. She had a vague memory of her house being at the edge of a field. It would just be a matter of knocking on a door and asking someone. In a village this small anyone could give her directions. But Libby felt daunted by the language difficulties. Besides, she'd been traveling for what seemed an eternity and all she wanted to do now was unroll her sleeping bag and crawl into it.

But, she couldn't sleep on the street, so . . . The house was about as accessible as a medieval fortress. She surveyed it critically, planning her siege. As there wasn't a staircase inside the house, each level had its own exterior door. Libby supposed that in the old days, families were loath to give up valuable indoor space to stairs. Maybe the key fit in a door on one of the other floors? Leaving her bags where she'd dropped them, Libby rose and grabbed the handle to the iron gate. Locked? How could that be? She was shaking on the handle in frustration when she noticed a shiny new padlock hanging from the inside. Clearly the old key in her hand didn't fit into that.

"Fine," she mumbled to herself, giving the gate a vindictive shake, "you want to be like that, be like that." There wasn't going to be anything easy about this trip. She might as well just resign herself to that fact and try to experience the adventure. Storm the ramparts.

She grabbed high on the curly design of the gate and hauled herself up. By the time she landed with a knee-jarring jump on the other side, her hands were covered with grime. She tromped up to the second level and frowned at the new-looking door. Who installed it? In fact, who put the padlock on the bottom of the stairs? The house was supposed to be empty, uninhabited since Nonna was young. Did they have squatters? Or maybe one of the relatives had moved in. Nonna's sister would have mentioned it, surely.

"Hello?" Libby knocked firmly on the door. Except for excited voices in the street below, all was quiet. To her uninitiated ear, perhaps Italians always sounded excited.

She continued on upward, turned the corner, and froze. This was not the view she remembered! There should have been a green panorama spread out before her. Instead, Libby looked down on the orange tile roofs of the street below. Jarred, she slapped a palm over her mouth. Right house position. Wrong street. Oops, she was trespassing.

So much for storming the castle. She bid a hasty retreat, scurrying down the stairs. Grabbing the gate, she began hoisting herself over. Two people stood on the other side. Libby had one leg over the top when the man asked her something. Libby had practiced how to say "I don't speak Italian" and it shouldn't have been a problem for her to just spout the words. But as soon as she looked down, her mind went blank. He had dark, curly hair and large brown eyes that, at that moment, were hooded with frowning eyebrows. Classically handsome, but with a tanned, rugged edge.

"I'm . . . so sorry." One leg in midair, winded, embarrassed—this was a wretched beginning. "Could you step back so I can jump down?"

One of those gorgeous black eyebrows rose. "What are you doing?" he asked in English.

"I have the wrong house. I'm sorry." She tried to smile, but her shoulder joint complained from the strain of holding her weight. "Please?"

The man shifted back and Libby landed with an un-ladylike grunt at his feet. When she teetered, he clutched her hand to steady her. Large, strong fingers led to a tanned, sinewy forearm, then a soft white shirt that draped over a muscular chest.

As a tall woman, Libby wasn't used to being eye-to-eye with a man's Adam's apple. She pulled her gaze away and pretended to brush the dirt off her slacks while she admired the rest of him. He wore scuffed canvas sneakers and well-worn jeans.

"The wrong house?" he asked.

His Italian accent made her want to melt into a puddle at his feet. She was exhausted. Puddles at feet wasn't her typical response. She cleared her throat. "Do you live here?"

"This is my, er, house," a middle-aged woman said in halting English. She had her fists braced on her narrow hips.

"I'm sorry," Libby said yet again. "I haven't been here in years and it appears I've gone one street too high."

At this, the woman narrowed her eyes. "Who are you?"

Libby jutted out her hand. "Libby Zufferlia." She decided they might know her full name so she added, "Elizabetta Zufferlia."

When the woman simply stared at Libby's hand, the man reached over and shook it. "I'm Marcello Iacome," he said, "and this is my aunt, Marana Iacome." He smiled at Libby, looked back at his glowering aunt, then chuckled.

"How do you do?" Libby said, drawing herself up. What a terrible start with the villagers. She'd made a spectacle of herself in a record-breaking five minutes. "I apologize for inconveniencing you."

As Libby started to collect her luggage, she tried to ignore the flurry of Italian between the two behind her. If only she'd had more time to brush up on the language.

"My aunt would like to know how long you will be staying in Croce."

"I'm not sure."

Marana nodded an abrupt good-bye and started to unlock the door. She said something over her shoulder to her nephew, then disappeared inside.

Yes, Libby thought, it's that easy when you have a key!

Still smiling, Marcello lifted Libby's largest suitcase and, ignoring the rolling mechanism, started along the footpath. "I will show you to your house."

She took a moment to admire his broad back and easy stride. "How do you know which house I'm looking for?"

His back muscles moved as he shrugged. "You are a Loszach."

"How did you . . . ? I mean, in a way. That was my grandmother's name before she married." She gave up trying to pull her midsize suitcase. The wheels just didn't work over the bumpy cobbles. "Even so, I happen to know there are a number of Loszach houses in this village. How do you know which one?"

"You are Mattia Loszach's granddaughter." He stopped and turned as if he'd just realized something. "Why are you taking your suitcases?"

"Why wouldn't I?"

"You're not planning to stay in the house, are you?"

"Yes, I am."

He shook his head. "No, I will take you to your Uncle Victor's house. Turn around." He waved his arm imperiously. "Back up the hill."

Libby automatically followed his commanding motion with her eyes and then shook herself. "I don't want to go there. I'm going to Nonna's house."

He looked amused again. "To sleep?"

"Perchance to dream." She laughed. "If I have to stay in a hotel, I'll spend too much time driving up and down the mountain."

He made no attempt to hide his grin. "You are going to sleep in the Loszach house. You know its, ah, history?"

"Yes."

"It is very dirty."

"I'll clean it."

"You'll be cold and uncomfortable."

"I brought a sleeping bag."

"And there are scorpions."

"Scorpions?" She scratched the back of her neck.

"And no toilet."

She'd completely forgotten the washroom problem. But when her family visited before, there was an outhouse that sat precariously on the edge of the cliff in the back garden. And of course they had the inn down in the valley where they retired each night to a hot bath. "I don't mind an outhouse."

"It is gone." His eyes twinkled.

"Gone?"

He made a sweeping motion with the flat of his hand. "Slid off the mountain."

Libby was too tired to fully enjoy the imagery, and it didn't help that Marcello thought the whole thing very funny. In fact, it steeled her resolve. She did have a clean sleeping bag. She'd been wilderness camping and it couldn't be harder than that. No doubt she would make do until she made other arrangements. After all, the house had running water, gravity-fed right from the mountain. A bit of soap and elbow grease and she would have the place spiffy in no time.

"I'm sure I'll be fine. Please, lead on."

He lifted his shoulders and palms in another expressive shrug. "It is your decision, of course."

The facade of the correct house didn't look nearly as welcoming as the one belonging to Marcello's aunt. Cobwebs draped these windows. The shutters were long gone; only metal hooks remained. A wrought-iron gate guarded the exterior stairs here as well, but it looked rusty and immovable. Libby kept the disappointment from her face as she stopped before the cracked and weathered door.

"Thank you for your help, Mr. Iacome."

"Marc," he corrected. "I will wait and see that your key works."

He stood close to her, to better see the lock, she assumed. Tired, grubby, and disappointed though she was, she couldn't help recognizing the sensuality radiating from him. He cocked one eyebrow and stood there, as if nothing else was quite as important as waiting for the outcome of the key slipping into the lock.

Chapter Two

"Well, there we are, then. Thank you so much for your help, Marcello."

"Marc," he corrected, again.

"You can just leave that there, Marc." She indicated the suitcase.

"Would you like me to wait while you look inside?"

"No. No, but thank you. I'm good to go."

He backed off, both palms up, as if she'd been abrupt. Perhaps she had, she thought, but she just wanted to stop this intense scrutiny. Save it for another day. She smiled up at him, determined to soften the moment. "Forgive me. It's been a long journey."

"I understand. *Ciao.*" He turned on his heel and half-jogged back up the alley across the street.

After Libby hauled her luggage inside and shut the door, she hovered there in the dark, dank-smelling kitchen, trying to get her bearings. She didn't remember it being so small. So stale. So sad. Not that she had actually ever slept in the house. As far as she knew, no one stayed there. Not since Nonna was a girl. And nothing seemed to have ever been stolen or vandalized. Libby had known about the house and the village all her life, and yet she was never given a clear explanation about why no one ever moved into these rooms. She supposed it had something to do with the complex inheritance laws of Italy. Or perhaps it cost too much to update the place? No bathroom. No hot water.

"This is temporary," she mumbled to herself. "Only temporary."

She swung back around and reopened the door to let in the light and air, then went from window to window shifting aside gauzy curtains that felt sticky with cobwebs and grime. The windows opened from the middle, like the pages of a book, and spiders scurried away as she scraped the swollen wooden frames over the stone casements. No screens here; apparently flying insects weren't an issue.

"Not so bad. Not so bad."

The last window she'd opened was above a deep enamel sink stained with rust and coated with cobwebs, dirt, and dead bugs, one of which was, she feared, a scorpion. Her hands were so grimy she held them like claws, away from her clothing.

Thinking she probably looked a mess, she went to a dusty mirror and frowned at the image. A sooty imprint of her own hand smeared her face. She looked down at her hands and remembered clasping one over her mouth when she had realized she was at the wrong house. Yes— the grime from the iron gate!

"Not so tired that I have absolutely no vanity." She laughed as she spoke to the empty room. Now she understood that man's, Marc's, amusement. She grabbed a tissue from her handbag and took a couple of meaningful swipes at the mark.

Marc had noticed the handprint on Libby's face. Now, as he retraced his steps back to his aunt's house, he smiled at the memory. Apparently people really did slap their hands over their mouths when startled. Whereas he found it amusing, he didn't think for one moment that Aunt Marana would agree. The Loszach house had been the stuff of whispers and sidelong glances his whole life and now, after all these years, someone planned to sleep there.

"There you are! What were you doing? Courting the girl? She's that Mattia Loszach's granddaughter, Marcello."

Marc made an effort to wipe the smile from his face. "She said her name was Libby Zufferlia."

Marana blew an exasperated breath through her closed lips. "What is she doing here?"

He shrugged and made a show of inspecting the gate that Libby had climbed over, giving the metal a firm rattle. The hinges embedded in the cement between the stones didn't look at all disturbed. Libby had a long, thin body, but she had substance the way an athlete did. He almost sucked in a breath at the memory of her shapely legs swinging down to the ground.

"Well?" Marana glowered at him as if Libby's presence were his fault.

"I don't know what she's doing here, but she plans to sleep in the Loszach house."

"For how long?"

"I don't know. I didn't ask."

She gave him a shove on his shoulder that didn't move him. "Go find out."

"You want me to spy for you?"

"This is no joke, Marcello Iacome."

He stared at his aunt for a long moment. Silver strands threaded through her hair but she was still a handsome woman. She glanced toward the corner leading down to the Loszach house. Marana was not a lighthearted or particularly emotional person, but clearly this situation had her worried.

"I'll make friends with her and—" Marc started.

"Don't make *friends* with her! You know how dangerous they are."

He bit back the urge to scoff at the word *dangerous*. The Mattia Loszach situation happened fifty years ago and Libby was not the same person as her grandmother. But then, character was in the blood. He patted his aunt's forearm reassuringly. "Acquaintances then. And find out what's going on."

She kissed him on the cheek. "You're a good boy, Marcello."

Twenty-nine years old and a foot taller than his aunt, and she still called him a boy.

Libby twisted open the rounded lever on the tap and waited. She expected to see water. Rusty colored, perhaps, but still water. When nothing happened, she looked under the sink. Unfortunately there didn't seem to be a shut-off valve. There was, however, a metal pail. She dumped out what she dearly hoped was a rotted rag and not a dead rodent.

She had a vague memory of a well in the village square. Perhaps it still worked? Or better yet, there might be a public tap somewhere. She closed the door behind her as she left the house and then started to the right, up the street. The back of her neck twitched as if people were watching. Without being obvious, she looked around at the balconies and open windows. They appeared empty. The other houses along this stretch also had doors that opened directly onto the street. Some of them were ajar. A waft of strong-smelling coffee had her mouth salivating. She heard what sounded like rapid-fire Italian from a radio and, as she neared the corner to the square, children's voices.

Libby paused to watch the scene. The well was still there, in the middle of the square. Three boys in short pants, a uniform of some sort, kicked around a ball. Two girls sat on the stone around the perimeter of the well watching them. Young people had probably been doing the same thing in this square for hundreds, perhaps thousands, of years.

Croce, 1944

Leopoldo Iacome's heart thudded as he watched a half-dozen boys scuffing and kicking at a leather ball. They hadn't seen him yet. His breath came in shallow gasps but he told himself it was from the steep hike through the woods path between the vineyard and the village, and not from fear.

The Croce boys laughed too loudly, Leo thought disdainfully. One of them even swore as the ball he'd booted ricocheted off the stone wall. They were performing for a small group of girls gathered by the communal well. His eyes flicked over them, appraising them. A couple of them were pretty enough, Leo saw, even though they wore old work dresses and flat shoes with socks puddling around their ankles. Not that he'd ever be interested in a village girl; Leo's family didn't have anything to do with mountain people. Croce people. At least, not in normal times.

Content in his family vineyards below, there were few occasions in Leo's life to come up to the village. Today as his eyes swept his surroundings, he noted its shabbiness. Evidence of the poverty, the strained circumstance left to them as their only spoils of war. The clothes and bedding suspended limp and dingy over lines strung between the balconies. The boys' shirts looked wrinkled and stained, and most of them didn't even fit well. Their pants hung too baggy and long, cinched at their waists as if they'd inherited from their fathers. Leo supposed that may be the case considering the number of men lost in the war. Other boys had cuffs so high above their ankles that they might as well have been wearing their short pants still. The morning air felt crisp, even cold, and yet a couple of the boys ran barefoot.

Leo looked down at his own clothing. Perhaps he should have worn something older? He thought he'd chosen casually enough, with an open-collar shirt and a vest. He stepped back around the corner of a building, bent down, and scooped some gritty dirt to rub the shine off his shoes.

He abruptly straightened and strode out into the square. He wouldn't linger in the shadows like a coward. How could he, an Iacome, be worried about what these scruffy boys thought of him? His country needed him. Didn't Il Duce tell them they all had to pitch in?

It was a boy about fourteen or fifteen years old, Leo's own age, who saw him first. He skidded to a stop and made a sound. In the sudden silence, Leo could hear the laundry flapping and slapping in the wind above. The ball rolled to a stop against the well casing.

Gerardo, the self-proclaimed leader of the group, was as tall and broad as a grown man, although Leo doubted that he had reached his sixteenth birthday. After a quick glance over his shoulder toward the girls, he swaggered forward. "What do you want?"

Leo marched across the square to meet him. "I want to help the Alpinis."

After a startled instant, Gerardo guffawed. The other boys quickly joined in.

Leo raised his voice. "I want to help our soldiers." When the noise quieted, he added, "You're helping them."

"You're just a kid."

"I can carry messages and collect firewood. I can do everything you do."

"We don't need your kind here."

"I'm Italian too. I have a right to—"

"You've got no rights here!" Gerardo interrupted, his hand extended, encompassing the village with one wide sweep. "Go home to your grapes." He grinned at his friends and they all started taunting.

"Yeah, go home."

"Get out of here."

"Maybe he's a spy!"

At that last comment, Gerardo's mouth dropped open. His eyes flashed fear, and then darkened to anger. "Are you a spy, Iacome?"

"Of course not!"

Leo kept his eyes pinned on Gerardo, but he could sense the other boys nearing, circling him. When Gerardo rushed forward, Leo braced himself, ready to jump aside. But someone kicked at the back of his leg so he crumpled. As Leo slumped to the ground, Gerardo kneed him in the chin and his head snapped back. Head reeling and tasting his own blood, Leo sprang quickly to his feet. But not soon enough. An avalanche of kicks and punches rained down on him. Through the boys' voices, he could hear a girl yelling.

"Stop it! Enough!" She waded into the fray.

Leo glimpsed her black hair and the faded blue of her dress. As Gerardo hauled back to aim another punch, his elbow hit the girl. Keeling in pain, she fell to her knees, her hands covering her face.

Without conscious thought, Leo shoved aside the boys who stood between him and the girl and dropped to his knees beside her. He expected to see tears when he gently pried her hands from her face. And perhaps a bloody nose. Instead, eyes bright with anger flashed back at him. A high, smooth forehead, satiny black hair, lips full and pink.

"Are you injured?" he asked, relieved that nothing was visible.

She gingerly felt her nose. "That hurt." Apparently assessing the damage to be slight, she leaned around Leo and glared at Gerardo. "You hit me!"

Evidently this girl had the power to cower even Gerardo. "I'm sorry. I didn't see you there." He jabbed a finger toward Leo. "It was his fault."

In an automatic response, Leo placed his hand at her elbow to help her rise. With an impatient movement of her arm and not a glance in his direction, she scrambled to her feet and began brushing the dust from her skirt. Something about the way her hand smoothed over her bottom had Leo's stomach tensing. But this beautiful girl seemed to have forgotten him.

"You could have just told him that the soldiers don't need any help. Or they're not here anymore."

"Mattia," Gerardo pleaded.

Leo admired the girl's profile. Mattia's profile.

Another of the girls appeared at her side and pressed the tips of her fingers on either side of Mattia's nose. With a shake of her head and only a subtle change to the lilt of her voice Mattia said, "I'm fine, Sophia. Thanks." But her voice to Gerardo was scathing. "You're such a clod."

At that, Gerardo shot Leo a poisonous glare that said *I'll get you for this.* "Leave our village, rich boy. And don't ever come back."

Bruised and bloodied, Leopoldo straightened his shoulders and turned on his heel to leave the village behind. It was then he realized that Mattia had pressed her hanky into his hand.

Croce, present day

Libby found a tap on the far side of the square cemented into the wall over a drainage grate. She half filled her bucket, rinsed it, and filled it again. She set the bucket aside and then ran the water over her fingers. When she splashed her face, the icy cold had her gasping. As she hadn't brought a towel with her, she hurried back to the house with water dripping from her chin.

Once inside, Libby set the bucket in the kitchen sink. Then she dipped the corner of her towel into the water.

"Hello?"

Libby yelped. "Oh! You startled me."

Marc leaned in the door but didn't step over the threshold. "Would you like me to turn on your water?"

She said hopefully, "You know how to do that?"

He smiled, but didn't look quite as amused has he had earlier. "I'll need the key to the cantina."

"The cantina?"

"Your cellar."

"Oh, well, I wonder . . ."

"Is that them?" Marc asked. Now he leaned in at an uncomfortable angle so he could look behind the door at the line of keys hanging there.

Libby gathered them up and followed around the side of the building and down a weed-choked opening to an ancient-looking door made of wide planks.

It was, she knew, tremendously lucky that he had come back. "Your English is excellent."

"Thank you. So is yours." His eyes twinkled as he pointed at her key ring. "I think it's that one."

After the door opened, he looked at her and indicated the cellar. *"Permesso?"* When she merely frowned, not understanding his meaning, he clarified, "May I enter?"

"Of course."

The cellar had a low ceiling and stone walls that were covered with a thin coating of cement, cracked and broken in places to expose the smooth stones beneath. A waist-high stack of firewood lined one wall. Good to know; she'd need wood for cooking and to heat water until she managed to get electricity and a stove. The solitary window had a board nailed across the frame so it couldn't be opened inward. Huge glass carboys for winemaking, an ancient watering can, handmade wooden sled, and mildewed cartons of what could be bottles of wine were mounded around. Libby promised herself that someday she'd explore down here. But not today.

"It's only cold water, right?"

He indicated the pipes. "Looks that way."

"You wouldn't happen to know any good plumbers, would you?" Now he turned his expressive eyes onto her.

"You are going to do some work on the house?"

"You said the outhouse fell off the mountain, so I think a bathroom is my first priority."

He grinned at her as he squatted next to a pipe.

"If it's only cold water," Libby asked, "why is it turned off down here?"

"It freezes sometimes in the winter." He applied force to a circular valve and the wheel creaked open. "Want to go up to see if it is working?"

"Sure."

As Libby scurried around the side of the building, she noticed that two people, a gray-haired man and an elderly woman wearing an old-fashioned housedress and headscarf, stood across the street looking toward the open door.

"Buon giorno," she called to them. The woman stared blankly, but the man's lips seem to move and he nodded a greeting.

Inside, Libby opened the tap and, after some rusty-sounding belches, the water gushed out. "It's working," she called.

Thinking that perhaps Marc wouldn't be able to hear

her voice through the thick wood of the floors, she hurried back outdoors. The couple still watched from across the street. They stood against a whitewashed wall and the sun, high in the sky, shadowed the lower half of their faces. Libby was debating going over to introduce herself when Marc joined her. As soon as the couple saw him, they silently moved down the street.

"Who are they?"

Marc wiped his hands on a handkerchief. "Signora Gorsha and her son. They live over that way. Probably interested to see who had opened the house. I expect they're distant relatives of yours, somehow."

"Relatives? More of the infamous cousins. Why didn't they come over?"

He shrugged his shoulders. "Saw me, no doubt."

"So? Are you a distant relative of mine?" she asked. Very distant, she hoped.

He stuffed the rag into his back pocket. "Me? No. I'm an Iacome. We're new to the village." Could it be that each time he spoke his name he actually stood a little taller?

She used this as an excuse to study him, the gorgeous long face and luscious brown eyes with the thickest lashes she'd ever seen. "I'm sure I've heard the name before, maybe when I was here with my nonna and my family a few years back."

"When I say new, I mean new in the way of this place. My great-great-grandfather bought the south side of the mountain."

"The whole south side of the mountain?"

"Good grape-growing slopes."

"Ting," she chimed, making the sound of a bell ringing. "The Iacome wines. Do you own that?" If so, he was filthy rich as well as handsome.

He chuckled. "Hardly mine. It's the family business, and there are a number of us." He looked up at the sky. "Speaking of which, I'd better get back to work."

"Thank you very much for your help, Marc."

"You're welcome. If you need anything, we're—" He stopped abruptly, as if he'd had a sudden thought. "Anyone can tell you where your relatives live."

The smile froze on Libby's face. She had assumed he was going to offer to help her himself; instead he made a point of sending her elsewhere. Well, fine. She'd see him around, probably, hopefully. For a chance meeting, he'd done plenty after all.

As she estimated that she'd been up for about thirty hours without sleep, not counting the couple of short naps on the airplane, Libby decided the first order of business was making a clean nest for herself to sleep in. She looked around the three crowded rooms of the first floor.

The house had been in the Loszach family for as long as anyone remembered. Since it had been built, probably. It perched on the lower edge of Croce, a tiny village on the side of a forested mountain in the Julian Alps. The building was actually divided down the middle: the right side had always been used as living quarters, and the left side as a barn to house the horses, chickens, and cows that the family had, in the past, depended upon for food and income. Libby knew that the uncles still used the barn side, which was why the roof had been maintained. Thanks to the solid roof and dry mountain air, the contents of the house were still usable, if dirty.

The kitchen had a tile stove pushed against a stone wall, a table in the middle of the room, a massive buffet, and a mishmash of wooden chairs. Farther inside, she found a sitting room consisting of a couple overstuffed chairs, heavy, carved furniture, and more closed cabinets. The room off that one, apparently an ample storage room, was filled with heaps of trunks and wooden crates. One side of this, Libby decided, would become the indoor bathroom.

She picked up the keys and went outside and up the exterior staircase to the first landing. A curious notion, she thought, to build a staircase on the outside. On that level she found two more rooms, each sparsely furnished with a narrow bed, a dresser, and a potbelly stove. A white porcelain chamber pot peeked from under a bed skirt. This would make a comfortable bedroom but she decided to see what the third floor had to offer.

As she pulled the second floor door closed and fumbled with the latch, the weight of exhaustion swept over her. She felt suddenly weepy and sad. How would she ever get this place livable for her grandmother in two months? There wasn't even any electricity, no hot water, and no bathroom—an oversight she was beginning to feel acutely. With a heavy sigh, she plodded up to the third floor and gasped.

The balcony was twenty feet long and ten feet deep, huge compared to the others in the village. It had a cement floor and a wrought-iron railing that looked powdery with rust. But the view. Oh the view. How had she forgotten? She stood still, with a hand flat on her chest, and breathed in the beauty of it.

Far in the distance spread the misty outline of the Adriatic Sea and the dim shape of islands where Venice waited. Closer in, the rolling hills gleamed with verdant spring colors. And in the valley cleft, she easily made out the ocher of the town, like a little teardrop, following the curve of the river. Closer still and to the right, softly undulating rows of grape trellises followed the contours of the mountainside. The Iacomes' no doubt. Two men walked down between the rows and, over to one side, a cluster of people—she couldn't tell their sexes from this distance—moved around a large machine of some kind.

She was still exhausted, but the sadness and tension rolled from her. She sank onto one of the stone benches that cupped a marble table, and leaned back to soak in the sun on her head, the breathtaking view, and the clean mountain air. It was to this beauty that her nonna wanted to return. But not the whole reason. She thought back to the conversation two short weeks earlier. What had her nonna meant by her *private* reason for wanting to return to Croce?

Two weeks earlier she'd been standing in her grandmother's living room.

"Of course a trip to Italy sounds great—" Libby had said.

"I'll pay all the expenses."

"And I want to help you, Nonna. I'm just not convinced you've thought this through."

With a familiar sniff, Mattia Zufferlia, Libby's grandmother, sat back in her chair and waited.

"Why don't we go back for a visit first?" Libby tried again. "We could stay in that town at the foot of the mountain."

"I've been for a visit. Now I'm moving back."

"But that was years ago, when Nonno was . . . still with us." Libby's grandfather had died a few short years earlier.

Mattia turned and looked toward the picture window and the manicured front lawn. The privet hedge was finally in leaf after a long winter. Beyond it, a car drove by at a sedate speed.

"Elizabetta, I'm moving back," she said softly. "I need your help." The use of her full name told Libby this wasn't a whim.

"But I don't want you to move away." And with that statement came the beginning of resignation. She knew her grandmother well. Nonna's mind was made up.

"I know, honey. I know," Mattia said softly. "But just think of the wonderful visits you'll have. You'll get to know your cousins."

Libby would try another tack. "Why to the village? Why not take an apartment somewhere modern? Somewhere with conveniences? You saw the house. It hasn't been lived in for something like fifty years." Go gently, Libby reminded herself. Her nonna was nothing if not fiercely independent.

"The house will need work," Mattia agreed.

"It'll cost a fortune."

Mattia raised one eyebrow, a smile playing at her lips. "You're worried I'm spending your inheritance?"

Libby laughed out loud at the old joke between them. "Yes, that's it, Nonna. I'm busted! See that lamp?" She pointed arbitrarily. "It's mine, I tell you. All mine!"

Amused but not sidetracked, Nonna continued, "Then it's that you begrudge giving your dear old grandmother one summer of your life?"

Uh-oh, she played the dear-old-grandmother card. Libby was sunk, so she sat.

"Of course I'll help."

The loose plans she'd made to go on a road trip for three weeks in June could easily be forestalled. They weren't carved in stone.

Mattia slapped her palms on her knees. "Then it's settled. You'll leave in one week."

"One week? I can't leave in one week."

"I'd prefer you left tomorrow, but I understand you have a job to finish. You did say the students are on work experience starting on Monday?"

"What is the rush?"

"I've been waiting all my life to move back to Croce."

Libby rolled her eyes. "This is the first I've heard about it."

"You will not use that tone of voice with me, young

lady." Grandmother and granddaughter locked eyes and smiled.

Using the arm of her chair for leverage, Mattia rose. She moved toward the mahogany sideboard. She was tall and elegant, with a sweep of salt-and-pepper hair brushed back from her face. Despite the age difference, the present-day Nonna didn't look so different from the portrait that hung on the wall. She'd been a young newlywed then, beautiful, serene, with her hand on her husband's arm. Admiring the elderly woman's inherent grace, Libby was always proud to be told that she had inherited her grandmother's satiny black hair, high forehead, and classic profile.

Her nonna was leaving them. Packing up and leaving. Why this sudden desire to leave her comfortable home of more than forty years, to move to a more-than-rustic Italian mountain village? Here, her children and grand-children all lived within an hour's drive. A seventy-two-year-old woman wiping the slate clean and starting all over?

"Of course, I'll have to put this house up for sale," Mattia said more to herself than to Libby.

"For sale?" Libby felt hollow.

"I'm sure it will be snapped up very quickly. This is a good neighborhood. Near the school."

"Oh, Nonna, I don't think there's any rush to sell the house. Why don't you see how things go?"

"I have enough money, not a bottomless supply of it, and the renovations will not be cheap." She smiled. "No, I'll call the real estate agent this afternoon."

Libby felt a tightness in her throat. What could she do? What could she say? This was her grandmother's house, her grandmother's life and, therefore, her grandmother's decision.

One more shot. "I'll make a deal with you." Libby was wringing her hands now as she paced. "I'll go to Italy for you. I'll check out the house and arrange the repairs. But on the condition that you don't sell this place until we see how things go over there."

Mattia took an envelope out of a drawer and returned to her chair. "Libby, my dear, I understand your confusion. But I promise you, I have a very good reason for moving back to Croce." When Libby opened her mouth to speak, Mattia held up a silencing finger. "A private reason, for now. Be assured, child, I have not lost my mind."

Nonna's eyes shone with something Libby couldn't quite read. Excitement? Certainly. And something else.

Libby took a deep breath. "My condition stands."

Mattia stared at her, considered the envelope in her hand, then looked up again. "Fine. It's a deal. Here's your ticket. You fly into Marco Polo Airport. The car reservation is in here too. I've already written to your Aunt Erika. She's sending a copy of the house key by courier."

Marc thought about Libby as he trod down the steep path from the village to his mother's home. So, this was the infamous Mattia Loszach's granddaughter. If Mattia had been as beautiful in her youth as Libby was now, he could easily believe the stories about her. Was Libby aware of the scandal? Even if she had heard, it was probably ancient history as far she was concerned. No matter if he disagreed with the practice, Marc knew fully that in a village like Croce, memories kept their strength for generations.

Of all the rotten luck, she'd have to be a Loszach! Try as he might, he couldn't see even the vaguest hint of the Loszach family in her. Loszachs tended to have square faces and deep-set eyes. Libby had an elegant face with an alabaster-smooth forehead framed in that gorgeous black hair . . . and those eyes, twinkling and so ready for fun. And, unlike the village Loszachs, she was tall and slender. And beautiful, despite the blue tinge under those eyes. He'd flown across the ocean enough times to know that the trip sucked the energy out of a person.

She might be beautiful, he reminded himself, but a Loszach was a Loszach. One couldn't fight generations of genetics.

He loped up the steps and swung open the door to his mother's house.

"Marcello!"

"Hello, Madre." He gave his statuesque mother a peck on the cheek.

"Have you eaten?"

"Yes."

"Pah, not enough. Look at you, all skin and bones."

When she squeezed his arm to illustrate her point, one of her eyebrows bounced up, as if impressed by his biceps. He chuckled. "I'm in a hurry, Madre. The truck's due back soon. I just dropped by to let you know that Aunt Marana wants to talk to you."

"What's the point of being the boss if you can't take time to eat? I have beautiful prosciutto."

Even though Marc liked the thinly sliced pork, he wasn't in the mood. "Maybe later."

"Sit. Sit. I want to talk to you. What do you want to drink? Corvina? Merlot?"

Knowing there was little point in trying to leave now, he wandered over to the large window overlooking the formal gardens of clipped hedges, statuary, and a fountain. "Whatever's open."

"Marana called a moment ago."

Ah, so that's why she was determined to keep him for a little talk. He turned back to the table. "So you know that Mattia Loszach's granddaughter is here."

Anna Iacome stopped her bustling. "But, why? Why is she here? Did she tell you?"

"She said she's staying in the house."

"That house? Stupid girl. For how long?"

"I don't know."

"You didn't ask? Marana told you to ask her. What did she say about her grandmother? About Mattia?"

"Nothing."

"Nothing?" she wailed. "How did you find out nothing? Marana told me you talked to her, even went around the outside of the house with her."

Marc released an offended scoff. "She was spying on me?"

Anna slapped down a platter of olives, cured meat, cheese, and bread. "You must have learned something."

"I think she's going to work on the house."

"Oh no," Anna said with a disappointed sigh. "Why?"

"I don't know."

"You should have asked. What if she's going to move here?"

Stalling for time, he popped a pitted olive into his mouth, chewed, and swallowed. "That's not likely. She doesn't know any Italian. Unless she's getting it ready for a summer house?"

"Not her! You know all too well whom I mean. Mattia. What if Mattia comes back?"

He pretended not to understand what she was implying. "What if she does?"

Anna sat down. "Marcello, this is serious. We can't have that woman back. Not after what she did."

"Madre—"

"I thought this would happen. Didn't I say so just the other day? Now that Leo is a widower, and Mattia is a widow . . ."

"Why does it matter? They're old."

"Not so old. Your grandfather is only seventy-four. That's not old. He will remarry." She pressed her thumb knuckle against her teeth for a second. "I have to get him interested in someone else before she gets here."

Marc chuckled and shook his head. "I'm sure you have someone in mind already."

Anna slapped her palm on the table. "You have to find out what this woman is up to."

He grinned. "That's no hardship. She's beautiful, just like you."

He was teasing her, as usual, but Anna, not in the mood for it today, remained stony faced. "She is a Loszach. I don't want you anywhere near her."

"Then how am I going to find out things for you?" He swirled the wine in his glass and sniffed its aroma. Young and uncomplicated but charming. He thought of Libby.

"You know exactly what I mean. That whole family is bad. They're not like us. Don't let her get her clutches into you. You keep your distance, Marcello."

"Because she might cast some sort of love spell on me?" he joked.

"I wouldn't put it past her."

"Nonsense."

"We don't believe in that foolishness, but they do. The Loszachs do. You just find out what they are planning, then stay away from her."

Marc didn't respond to this order, and he kept his concern to himself. These days the Loszachs didn't cause serious harm—name-calling, a few drunken brawls, vandalism—but it wasn't always that way. He thought about the sorrow he'd always felt in his grandfather and how it was caused by the Loszachs. He didn't like to generalize. Not all Loszachs were bad, obviously. But it was only prudent to keep them at arm's length.

Chapter Three

Libby was humming. There was a certain kind of joy in performing the most simple of tasks. She swished the rag into the icy water, squeezed the excess, and plopped the soapy cloth onto the kitchen table. Once damp, the wood's beautiful grain popped out. What was it? Walnut perhaps? Each board was more than twelve inches wide. Obviously a lovely kitchen table wasn't on her list of priorities, but someday Nonna had to get this beauty refinished.

She stopped in midswath when a rap sounded at the open door. A woman smiled at her shyly. She had black hair, cut in a bob, a square face, and wore a crisp white blouse tucked into a pair of twill slacks.

"My name is Vivia. I am your cousin." She spoke in the halting way of one uncertain of the foreign words.

"Please, come in." Libby was delighted. She moved

toward the other woman, uncertain how to greet a family member. They settled on joining hands and touching cheeks. Libby now wished she had lit the stove so she could offer her cousin some tea or coffee.

With a hand on her heart, she said, "I'm Elizabetta. But please call me Libby."

"Zufferlia. Yes. My grandmother and your grandmother, sisters," Vivia said.

"*Scusa. Non parlo italiano.*" Libby determined at that moment that during her time in Italy she would learn as much of the language as she could.

Vivia waved away Libby's concern. "Not important. I want to practice the English."

Vivia looked around the room, then grimaced at Libby woman to woman, commiserating rather than condemning the state of the dirty surroundings. "You have had breakfast?"

Libby thought about the energy bar and bottle of water she'd consumed at the crack of dawn three hours earlier and shook her head. "Not really."

"You come to my house, yes?"

"Now?" Libby looked down at her old sweatshirt and jeans. Did she want to meet her relatives looking like this? On the other hand, they might as well get to know the real Libby right from the start.

"Come. Come. We will have the *caffè*."

Real Italian coffee. She almost whimpered at the thought. "Okay. I'll just lock up."

"No bad person will come to your house."

Probably not, Libby thought, here in a village where

eyes watched her every move. She only had to look around at the crowded belongings that had stayed untouched here, in an empty house, for a half a century.

As they strolled along the streets, Vivia asked, "You have been to Croce before?"

"Years ago, with Nonna and my *madre* and *padre* and my—" Pausing, she struggled to recall the word for *brother*. "And my brother." The two women smiled together.

"Oh, yes. I am sorry." Vivia slapped her forehead, remembering the last visit. "You were a little child and I old. Older."

As they cleared the corner and started up the hill, Montagna Croce suddenly filled the skyline, rugged cliffs of pale rock, small outcroppings with what appeared to be stunted trees and brush, and great black crevices. At this time of year, the top of the mountain looked like a bumpy, bald head. No snow-capped peaks here. She wanted to stop and gulp it all in, the staggering, overwhelming mass of it, but her cousin continued striding up the street.

"It's so beautiful here."

Although Vivia shrugged as if indifferent to the compliment, she smiled, pleased. They traveled up a steep, rocky path between two other buildings. When the space widened, they faced the paved area where people in the locale parked their cars. The village dated back to long before automobiles, so the narrow streets and lanes weren't wide enough to drive upon.

"That is the bakery," Vivia said with pride, pointing to

the long, two-story stone building with dozens of windows and bright white-washed walls.

"The Loszach Bakery," Libby said to explain she knew about the famous family business. She'd smelled the sweet spicy aroma since she woke up. It was comforting and familiar because Loszach gubana were a treasured family tradition as she was growing up. Her nonna received a parcel of those cakes every Christmas. Together with the Iacome winery, these two enterprises were the largest employers in this area. It seemed everyone worked for one or the other.

"It's a lovely building."

"The paint . . . we must clean it always. Those bad children from down." Vivia gestured behind her.

"Do they . . . ?" Libby pantomimed someone painting graffiti.

"*Sì*. And they throw the rocks."

"They break the windows? How awful. Very bad."

"Ach, Iacome."

Marc's handsome face flashed in her mind. She couldn't picture that cultured man throwing rocks through windows. But when he was a child? "Why do they do that?"

Vivia shrugged. "Always Loszach and Iacome . . ." She raised her hands in claws facing one another and growled.

"Even in Nonna's day? When Nonna lived here?"

"*Sì, sì*."

Libby slowed her step and tried to imagine the bakery

as it was in her grandmother's youth. The war had just ended so they didn't have much money. Certainly the building wouldn't have been freshly painted. Perhaps it had never been painted then, but was just gray-brown field stones. The graffiti was likely done with chalk rocks, not paint. Were the parents preoccupied with trying to come to grips with the ruin in their lives that the war had caused? Did they allow their children to run wild? No, probably the children had more responsibility then. So many men had died. So much suffering.

"During the war," Libby asked, thinking that a common enemy may have united all the people in the area, "did the village people get along with the people down below? With those in the vineyard?"

Vivia shot her an incredulous look. "No!"

Before Libby had a chance to respond, they'd reached Vivia's house. She lived in a narrow building with vines growing up the walls. The door stood welcomingly open.

Although very small, it was scrupulously clean and tidy. The lace framing the windows looked handmade. A jar of spring wildflowers sat in the middle of the small table. The cozy six-foot-by-six-foot living room was large enough to hold only a love seat, armchair, and small potbelly stove. For a brief moment, Libby had entertained the idea of camping out at her cousin's house until she got a bathroom installed, but the length of the love seat quickly put a halt to that scheme.

Vivia went through the ritual of making the coffee in

the effortless way of one who'd done it all her life: grinding the beans, filtering the coffee, and finally, frothing the milk with an ear-splitting machine.

"Is your husband at work?" Libby asked.

"I am unmarried. To the great sorrow of our family." Her ease told Libby that this woman would marry when she wanted to and not a moment sooner.

"I work in the bakery," Vivia continued. "I do the . . . er . . . accounts. You work?"

Libby put a teaspoon of sugar in her coffee, something she'd made herself quit in Canada. But coffee here would be, she knew, stronger. "I teach."

"The school year is over for you? In May?"

"This kind of school is. I teach young adults in a college."

The women chatted as best they could over the coffee, even managing to share a laugh at Vivia's energetic impression of some of the aunts and uncles Libby had yet to meet.

At the beginning of the visit, it was a struggle at times to follow Vivia's accent, but Libby soon picked up on the music in the speech, the nuances, the raise of an eyebrow or the stressing of a word, and understanding came more easily. Nevertheless, she imagined that speaking a foreign language to someone you didn't know was exhausting, so she didn't stay long.

As she strolled back toward her house, Libby thought about her cousin and the shared genes. They were, in fact, second or third cousins, but here in Croce the distinctions blurred. Perhaps there was something to that family-bond theory; she and Vivia felt comfortable with each other right away. She looked forward to getting to know her over the next couple of months. It was easy to picture Nonna and Vivia becoming friends too, and that was a comfort to Libby.

As she stepped around a corner and heard a clear *coo-coo, coo-coo,* she automatically glanced around for a village clock.

"It's not a clock," Marc said from where he sat on the rounded marble slab that marked the step to her gate.

Her heart gave a little start. "Excuse me?"

He stood and brushed dust from the rear of his jeans. He wore a loose, canvas-type jacket with a T-shirt underneath. "It's a bird. I saw you look for a clock."

"It sounds just like one," she stammered. The man just stood there all handsome and smiling, the breeze tossing his brown curls around his forehead. For a reason that had nothing to do with exercise, she had trouble catching her breath.

"I expect the clock sounds just like the bird." He grinned.

"Right, right."

"I brought us some coffee and pizzelles." He indicated the paper bag at his feet.

He said *us*. He meant to visit awhile. The dank interior of the house wasn't ready for company just yet so she suggested, "Let's go up to the balcony."

"The famous balcony," he said.

"Famous?"

"I can see it from my vineyard. It looks inviting."

When Marc placed his hand on the small of her back to guide her toward the staircase, Libby felt like leaning into it. She wanted to touch him, to have him touch her. "I'm assuming the balcony is safe. I plan to get a structural engineer or someone to check it out."

"I don't think you need to worry about it. There was a huge earthquake here in '76. Everything was checked and strengthened then."

"That was a long time ago."

"These houses were built to last centuries."

At the landing to the second floor, Libby paused and turned to look back. She'd been so enamored of the view down the mountain that she hadn't even considered if there was a similarly astonishing one looking upward from the house. Beyond the buildings and the rooflines above them, the mountains filled the sky. The vastness of them, the weight of stone, was beautiful and awe-inspiring.

"It makes my heart race," she whispered to Marc, who stood one step below her so that their faces were level.

His eyebrows rose as he nodded. "I like this view just as much, perhaps more, than the valley. Have you been to the top?"

There was, she knew, a path from the end of the road to the rounded top of the mountain. "Not since I was a kid. I remember the view from up there though, the snow-capped peaks in the distance."

"Would you like to go again? Tomorrow morning, perhaps?"

She hesitated. Was he asking her on a date? She recalled the way Vivia grimaced when she spoke of the Iacomes. And then there was the scandal in the misty recesses of her own family's history. Did that have something to do with her nonna's desire to return to the village? It occurred to her that it had been good luck to run into Marc Iacome on her first day in the village. He could probably shed some light on the Nonna situation. But she'd have to tread carefully. She glanced back up at the mountain, at its daunting slope, and had another thought.

"I would like that," she said, "but I'm not as fit as you. I would hold you back." He'd probably jog up the mountain whereas she'd be gasping every step. Not an attractive sight.

"It is hard for those not used to our thin air."

What a gracious way for him to respond to her rejection. On the other hand, maybe he was backpedaling? Did he regret asking her? "Yes, I'd better acclimatize myself for a few days first."

"Of course." He motioned for her to continue up the stairs.

Once she had her face turned away, Libby grimaced. She'd handled that very poorly.

After Marc took a moment to admire the view from the top, he settled on a bench and unpacked the bag: two mugs, a stainless-steel thermos, and a clear sack of cookies he had called pizzelles. The last thing he withdrew was a legal-size envelope stuffed with papers.

He slid the envelope toward her. "These are left over from when I helped my aunt renovate her house. The one we caught you breaking into."

"Breaking into!"

He squeezed her forearm, sending tingles along her skin. "I'm teasing, I'm teasing. I know it was an honest mistake."

Libby relaxed and laughed. She fingered open the envelope. It contained shiny brochures with luscious photos of everything from bathtubs to gas cookers. "This is so thoughtful. Thank you." She leafed through the sheets, stopping at an apron kitchen sink. "Aren't these gorgeous? Did your aunt renovate her whole house?"

"Had to. She rents to people who like to hike the mountains, but are used to luxury at the end of the day."

She sat up, excited. "Rents? It's a rental property? Is anyone staying there now?"

He looked suddenly wary. "No. But it gets busy in a couple of weeks."

"This is perfect. Obviously Nonna didn't know about the house. I suggested renting right away, of course, but she was certain that no one did that in Croce. I suppose they didn't before. But she could come and see if she really wants to move back before we spend all her money on restoration. I'll call your aunt to see about renting it."

"No," he said quietly.

"But you said it was empty now."

"She's not renting it right now." He looked away, toward the valley below.

She didn't like the guilty shadow in his expression. "Why not?"

"If it were up to me . . . ," he said with a shrug and both palms turned up.

So, the Iacomes didn't want to rent to the Loszachs. Even though she'd half expected that to be the case, she felt frustrated. It was going to be difficult living in her nonna's house while it was under renovation. It appeared that Marc's aunt's house was in the village. Apparently some Iacomes lived amid Loszachs, physically together but socially separated. How very strange.

Libby decided she'd find Marc's aunt and ask about the rental property herself. With a slight cringe, she thought back to the way that Marana had treated her when they were introduced. With scorn. It wasn't exactly a good first impression. But then, Libby had been trespassing on Marana's property. Surely Marc had explained the whole misunderstanding. Also, she might be receptive to a personal appeal, and Libby knew she could be quite persuasive. She unscrewed the top of the thermos and breathed in the heady aroma. Another cup of coffee? Sure.

"Is Marana your father's sister?" she asked.

"She married my uncle."

"Ah, so she is an Iacome by marriage." Now she knew what last name to look for: Marana Iacome.

He nodded. "They've been married so long that she's one hundred percent Iacome now." Changing the subject, he nodded toward the treats he brought. "I hope you like these cookies. My mother made them."

Libby wondered at the phrase *one hundred percent Iacome*. Curious choice of words.

While they nibbled on the cookies and sipped coffee, Libby flipped through the brochures. They were written in Italian, but she was able to compare styles and approximate prices. The trick, she decided, was to choose appliances and fixtures that weren't glaringly modern, so they wouldn't appear too out of place in the ancient house. Quality, but not extravagance. They need not be large either, as only one person would likely be using them. Sturdy and functional, without the bells and whistles of electronic gadgets.

She stopped at a whole brochure about black plastic pipes and sighed heavily. Picking out fixtures and appliances was one thing, but what did she know about plumbing and electrical work? Now that she had seen the house, she knew the job was much more than cleaning and decorating. She needed a contractor.

She glanced at Marc and her mind immediately veered off. He leaned back against the building, his long legs stretched out before him and he gazed toward the panorama. The soft fabric of his shirt draped over the contours of his chest. He must have sensed the way she studied him because one side of his sculptured mouth turned up in a smile. *Where is my camera?* Libby mused. *What a picture he makes.*

"That was a big sigh." Only his eyes turned in her direction.

Better and better, she thought, meeting his gaze. On to business Libby, she warned herself. She waved at the brochures. "This is all very daunting to me. I've never had to buy anything like this, you know, like a sink or a stove. Never mind discussing wiring and plumbing. Is there even a sewage system here?"

He shook his head. "You'll need a cistern."

"A what?" The word sounded vaguely familiar. She covered her face in her hands and spoke through her fingers. "How did Nonna expect me to pull this off?"

"Pull it off?"

"Succeed. I'm really not qualified."

"I have a friend who—" He frowned and glanced back toward the view.

"Who what?"

Marc shifted around so his knees were under the table. "There's something I should . . . I hesitate to even mention it because you'll find it all very old-fashioned. The thing is, the Iacome family and the Loszach family don't get along."

Although she'd heard as much from Vivia, she kept her face placid. "Don't get along?"

"It's been going on for generations. It probably started a hundred or more years ago, but it flared up again because . . . well, in the years after the war."

"And that affects me how?"

"It affects us both. For example, my friend—my second or third cousin, Enzo—would be a perfect person for you to hire to oversee the work. But if he helped you, he'd be in trouble with his mother, and aunt and— Well, you see my point?" As he spoke, his long, tanned fingers moved eloquently.

"Not really," she replied. "How old is this Enzo? Let's see if I have this straight. If I hired a grown man to do a job for me his mama and auntie would get mad at him?" She chuckled.

Marc did not.

"You're serious, aren't you? Is that why you think your aunt won't rent her property to me?"

He tilted his head apologetically. "I didn't lie to you. She's not renting right now."

"Let me understand you. Even if she did want to rent the house right now, she wouldn't rent it to me because my grandmother was born a Loszach and I am a Loszach by blood?"

"I'm sorry." He lifted his chin. "We are Iacomes. That is the way of this place."

Libby sat straight. "You're completely serious, aren't you? What does she think? That anyone in my family would wreck the place or something?"

"No, no. It's a matter of pride . . . well, not pride . . . tradition."

Libby found this all vaguely amusing as well as irritating. "So this *feud,* how does it manifest itself?"

He shook his head slowly as if to say, "I don't understand."

Libby clarified, "What has happened? Has a Loszach dumped gravel on Iacome land? Or an Iacome cut down a Loszach tree?" She couldn't picture anything more serious than that.

Now he looked a bit insulted. "No. People are polite. But they don't do the business with one another."

"I can't wrap my head around this." He tilted his head in question so she rephrased. "Let me understand this. Does this mean we don't buy your wine and you buy your baking from another bakery? Is there another bakery?"

Silence reigned until Libby asked quietly, "Does this second or third cousin of yours need the work? Is he available? Is he good?"

"Yes, yes, and yes. But you're missing the point."

"Maybe he doesn't care about the so-called feud? Why don't I ask him? After all, you don't seem to mind being near me."

He shot her the crooked smile again. "Me, personally? No. But my mother, for instance, she would never be your friend."

"And your aunts would never be my friends."

"Exactly."

"Marc." Taking a calming breath, she said, "We have an expression in English: *Never say never.*" Libby looked at the house, at the handmade orange tiles on the roof and the multiple panes of wavy glass on the windows. It seemed very ancient and traditional to her, so perhaps it wasn't totally beyond belief that a feud still existed here in Croce.

"Marc, I need advice. I need help." She gave him her most pleading look. "Could you just ask your cousin to come up here for a consultation? I'll pay for his time." She had a sudden thought. "Does he speak English?"

"Very poorly."

She considered him. "How is it that you speak English so well?"

"Went to school in California."

"California? Why there?"

"I learned English, and I got to spy on the competition. Californian wines are cutting into our market."

"So, your friend . . . ?"

Marc stood and walked to the edge of the balcony and leaned slightly over the railing. "I used to play down there in the woods when I was a boy."

"If he could just give me some advice?" she persisted, thinking Marc was trying to avoid answering.

"I suppose Enzo and I *could* approach from down there, where we wouldn't be noticed."

She shot him an incredulous look. "Kind of juvenile, don't you think?"

"If you knew the women in my family, you'd agree there's a need for, ah, subtlety. They are formidable, to say the least." Humor and affection shone in his eyes.

She glanced at the brochures and thought again about how incompetent she was when it came to things like—what was the word he used?—cisterns. What the heck was a cistern? "I don't want you to lie for me, but I really need help."

"I never lie." He grinned, his teeth white against his tanned face. "I evade questions."

Suddenly, his expression sobered. He shifted to stare down toward his own lands. His strong, lithe back straightened and his chin lifted. Watching him, Libby felt a painful catch in her throat.

Marc pulled out his cell phone and punched in some numbers. After a moment, he spoke in a flurry of Italian.

With a rush of relief, Libby dragged her hands through her hair.

"He can come tomorrow," Marc said with hand over the phone.

"That's wonderful. Thank you so much." They settled on a time.

As Marc didn't seem to have any qualms about the strength of the balcony, Libby joined him at the far end. The structure itself was only three stories from the ground, but the fact that it sat on the edge of a clifflike incline made it feel as if it hung in midair. She took a moment to regain her equilibrium and then looked over the edge. Immediately below was what remained of a cobbled courtyard surrounded by a knee-high stone wall. Vines almost obliterated the wall and weeds grew through the stones.

"You're going to come up the hill that way?" she clarified, looking at the dense growth beyond the courtyard.

"I'll bring a machete." He chuckled.

That morning, the distant view had been obscured and, even now, with the clouds blown clear, the mist hid the farthest places. However, the nearby Iacome vineyards were easy to pick out. In one spot, some kind of machine moved slowly between the rows. In another place, two men appeared to be pruning. From this height, they looked like toys.

"Well, I'd better be getting back to work." He also looked toward his property.

"Would you like a tour of the house?" she asked quickly. Anything to keep him around a bit longer.

"I would, but not right now." He reached over and tilted the watch on her wrist so he could read it. "I'm due back."

When his eyes locked with hers, she was sure he could feel her blood quicken in her pulse. She hardly dared to breathe. Marc broke the connection first.

"*Allora* . . ." He stretched the word into a sigh.

"Yes, well . . ."

Now Marc looked extremely pleased with himself. "*Ciao,* Libby."

She watched him bound down her stairs like a kid leaving for summer vacation and then she dashed inside to look up *allora* in her Italian dictionary. There, in black and white, she saw it basically translated to "then." Libby had a feeling, though, that when Marc Iacome said it, it had an altogether different meaning.

Chapter Four

A little while later, Libby dithered in the middle of the room rubbing her hands together. Where to start? She wanted to clean the kitchen, if only to make one place comfortable. On the other hand, Marc's cousin was coming the next morning. She should at least have a rough idea of what kinds of things to discuss with him.

Nonna would need a smallish propane stove. Or did they use gas here? And hot and cold running water in the sink, a fridge, electric lights, and outlets.

Could Nonna be happy here? Would she be safe and comfortable and not lonely? She did have family in the village. Libby sighed as she admitted to herself that it was very possible that her grandmother would be happy here, that her own aversion to the idea was purely selfish. Even when Nonno was alive, her grandmother had been independent. Her own woman. And she taught Libby to

51

think for herself as well. As she glanced around, Libby allowed her imagination to take over. She could envision this house complete. Fixtures. Curtains. Furniture. Art. Yes. This could be a charming home for Nonna, and she resolved to do her level best to see that everything was *perfetto* by the beginning of July.

The floors throughout the house could use a sanding and finishing, but first things first. Compared with the kitchen, the sitting room required very little work besides electricity. Nonna would need an indoor staircase too. Otherwise, she'd have to leave her bedroom, go outdoors and down the stairs, and come inside again just to use the facilities in the middle of the night. Besides, hadn't Marc said it got cold enough here to freeze pipes? Libby appreciated that it was an architectural design typical to the area and that countless other senior citizens made out just fine. But she had no problem rationalizing the expense since Nonna hadn't grown used to it over time. In fact, her grandmother had been younger than Libby was now when she last lived in Croce.

Croce, 1946

Mattia Loszach pleaded with one palm outstretched. "It's winter, Padre. I have no coat."

Even her meek mother tried to intercede. "In these times . . . with the war . . ."

The war had changed Croce from a thriving village to an enclave of the needy. With the cattle slaughtered, the dairy filled with dust. With the fields reduced to barren waste, there was no grain for the bakery. People barely held on to their lives.

"She can wear a blanket," Josk Loszach bellowed.

"You want me to freeze."

"I want you to tell me where it came from!"

"It was a gift."

"A gift?" He lowered his eyebrows. "Who gave you that coat?"

Mattia held her chin raised but she could feel the heat of a blush creep up her throat. Her knees trembled.

"Well? Well?" The truth dawned on her father's face first. "*Madre di Dio.* It's that boy."

Both parents stared at her in horror. "You've been seeing an Iacome."

"He's a nice—"

Her father backhanded her across the side of the head. "What did you give him in return?"

The shock, more than the pain, had her gasping. "Padre! Nothing!"

He yanked at the coat but Mattia clutched the soft wool to her chest. Her mother screamed and beseeched. Josk stomped to the door, dragging her along. Her fingers ached and she cracked her shin on the door frame, but she wouldn't release her hold on the coat, a gift from Leopoldo Iacome.

"He said they weren't using it. They have lots of coats."

"Of course they do! Collaborators, every last one of them! The war made them rich."

Mattia was appalled. "Never!"

He dragged her along the road, down the cobbled alley, and onto the woods path. A few yards along, she caught the toe of her right foot on a root and fell with an oomph. Her throbbing fingers released the precious fabric.

"Please don't do this, Padre. Please."

"Enough!"

Mattia crumbled there on the frozen earth. She felt her mother brush past her, and then saw other legs, skirts, and trousers. Had the whole village witnessed this?

"Here, Mattia." Sophia, her best friend, helped her stand. "Oh, you've torn your dress."

Dirt, twigs, rotted leaves smeared her elbow, hip, and leg. A slice of fabric had torn. She clutched her aching elbow, winced at the sting, and pulled away her hand wet with blood. Sophia tried to turn her back up the path, but Mattia shook her off. Limping, she struggled to catch up to her father.

How could he think those horrible things? She remembered a day long ago when Leo Iacome had come up to the square asking if he could help the Alpini. Would someone do that if his family collaborated with the enemy? No! Now that she knew him, the very idea was ludicrous. Good, strong, kind Leo.

As she cleared the woods, Mattia saw her father. "Padre, stop!"

His strong legs carried him along a row of vines and then he swung out of sight. She ran, whimpering, to stop him. The clump of villagers who had followed allowed her to pass.

Mattia's father faced off with Leopoldo's father. Josk Loszach against Basilo Iacome. The Croce baker against the wine producer. Although Josk stood a head shorter than the lanky Iacome, he was thick with muscles.

"We don't want this!" Josk threw the coat on the ground.

Basilo Iacome nudged it with a boot. "What is this . . . thing?"

"I warned you to keep your people away from Croce."

"Bah! We have no need of Croce." He sneered and waved a dismissive hand. "Leave. Go back up the mountain."

"Your filthy son! Tell him to keep his hands off my daughter."

"You dare insult my son!"

The yelling brought workers running. Some held pruning shears; others came with only their fists. Mattia looked around wildly for someone to intervene before a fight broke out. But the Croce men looked equally ready to bloody their knuckles.

"You can't control your own—"

"My son has done nothing!"

"If he goes near my daughter—"

"Your daughter! You flatter yourself."

"You deny he gave this coat to her?"

Mattia felt mortified. She shoved through the growing crowd and grabbed for her father's arm. "It's nothing. I don't need it. Padre, please . . ."

"Her?" Basilo Iacome rudely looked her up and down. "He wouldn't bother."

Josk Loszach's mitt of a fist smacked Basilo square on the chin. The screaming and yelling started before the two men hit the dirt.

Suddenly Leo Iacome vaulted through the melee. He made a grab for his father and hauled him to his feet. Mattia shook her mother and Sophia loose, intending to do the same, but her father had already sprung up. Basilo swiped his forearm across his face, leaving a smear of blood on one cheek. Like a bull on a charge, he butted Josk in the gut.

In a rush, the men were upon one another. Croce men against Iacome men: smashing noses, kicking ribs, pulling hair. The women scrambled backward.

Mattia looked up and saw Leo's anguished eyes boring into hers. Someone swung a punch at him. He lifted a forearm to block it, turned, and joined his father in battle.

"Leo?" Mattia whimpered.

"What did you expect him to do?" Sophia snapped. "It's his family."

The women trudged back up to the village to unearth their bandages from the chests and to put water on to boil. There would be broken bones to set that night. They knew all about fixing their men's bodies.

Croce, present day

Libby climbed over the dusty chests and crates intent on measuring the space off the sitting room. It appeared long enough for a full bath and wide enough to house the washer and dryer too. She wondered whether the local people used electric or gas dryers. Perhaps neither; almost all the balconies had specially tiered gadgets to work as clotheslines.

An hour later, she pulled on a brass handle until the trunk it was attached to scraped across the floor and out into the sitting room. She stumbled back a few steps and sprawled in the soft armchair. She'd begun with the intention of measuring the storeroom's walls, and ended up pulling everything out. Now only a narrow path led to the empty room. She had to find somewhere to put it all. The second floor? She groaned. The trunks would have to be emptied and their contents brought up bit by bit.

On the other hand, the chance to sift through antiques and memorabilia held a lot of appeal. Some of the everyday items lying around the old house were hundreds of years old. Clearly Europeans had a different notion of history than North Americans. At home, something two hundred years old was cherished, restored, and maintained for its historic value. Here, Libby thought wryly, a grudge could be held as long.

When her stomach grumbled, she decided it was time to make the trip down the mountain to buy groceries. A stop at a restaurant sounded lovely too. Nonna had supplied her with a few maps before she left Canada: one of Italy, one of the northeastern section, and lastly, a huge, heavy-duty topographical map that clearly marked the roads zigzagging over the mountains. Libby unfolded the big one on the kitchen table and charted a course for the nearest town of any size: Cividale. She tried to sound out the name in Italian: Chi-va-dal-eh.

The map displayed Croce as a little cluster of a few dozen black squares, so it was easy to pick out her house on the lane curving around the lower edge of the village. Physically, the mini-village of buildings representing the Iacome land almost abutted Croce, but it could only be accessed by a road that cut off the main one going down to the valley. It seemed that nothing connected it to the village, although they shared the same little mountain ledge. Or more likely, she thought, the wooded paths were just too small to show up on even this detailed map. Still, it seemed odd.

Presumably, she'd be able to find Marc's aunt in a house down there, and ask her about the rental property. But that chore could wait until later in the day.

Libby washed up, changed clothes, and left her door unlocked. Even though she considered herself to be a brave person, the thought of driving alone down the mountain to find a grocery store made her twitchy with anxiety. Everything felt so unfamiliar and complicated. That's why, during her visit that morning, she had gratefully accepted Vivia's offer to drive her to town.

The breeze must have been blowing just right because the streets of Croce were sweet with the spices from the bakery. Libby remembered a friend from back home who once had a flat above a coffee roaster. Even the days when the aromas seemed slightly burned and bitter, there was a comfort in the smell. Libby felt a tug of homesickness, which she quickly shook off.

Her step slowed at the sounds of rough shouting,

quickly identified as children fighting. Up ahead, a girl darted from her doorway and flew up the street, her sneakers slapping on the cobbles. By the time Libby reached the parking area, a dozen youngsters ranging from six or eight to teenagers circled two boys fighting. She wondered if she should intervene. Then a man came out of the bakery swinging a broom.

"Basta! Basta!"

At first the youngsters tried to ignore him, but when he started thumping his broom on the combatants' backs, they pulled apart.

Libby felt like someone rubbernecking at a traffic accident so she continued on to her cousin's house.

Ten minutes later, Libby sat in the passenger seat of her cousin's tiny car with her hand clutching the grab bar above her shoulder. They swerved one bend and her body weight slung to one side; they swerved the next bend, and her weight flung to the other side. If it hadn't been for the seat belt, she'd have landed in Vivia's lap.

Then the side of the road ended in a sheer drop. "Whoa," Libby squealed.

"Scusi. I frighten you?"

"I'm just not used to the Italian way of driving." As they turned yet another corner, she glimpsed a mountain village in the distance, but only saw it long enough to register the tile roofs and a church steeple with an oversize cross.

Vivia may have relaxed her foot on the accelerator; it was hard to tell. When they reached a relatively straight

section, Libby pried her fingers from the strap. It occurred to her that a break in the trees that had just blurred
by might have been a road.

"Is that the way to the Iacome place?"

"Yes."

"What's it like down there?"

Vivia shrugged. "You can see it from Croce. The
grapes, the houses."

Libby watched her cousin's profile. "Do you go there
very often?"

Vivia released both hands from the steering wheel and
made a disgruntled motion. "Pffft. No one goes there."

"Marc told me the Iacomes and the Loszachs don't
get along."

Now Vivia did slow down. "Marc?"

"Marc Iacome. I ran into him yesterday."

She explained how she'd been caught climbing over
the gate of the wrong house.

"No, is not true!" Vivia howled in a remarkably deep-
toned laugh. Then she wheezed out, "Marana Iacome?"

Grinning, Libby nodded. "Yes. Marc's aunt."

Vivia caught her breath. "Ah, is very funny."

"Marc thought so, but his aunt looked angry."

She sniffed. "Yes, of course."

"You sound as if you don't like Marana Iacome."

Vivia glanced at Libby. "I know her only a little." She
nodded toward the turn ahead. "We are in the valley now.
See this? You watch for this."

Libby understood that Vivia meant that she should
note the landmarks so she could find her way when she

drove to town alone. She craned her neck to look at the sign from the other angle. "It says Slovenia that way," she said, surprised. "Is there a border crossing?"

"Not anymore, no. The farmers, they go to their fields there, come home at night."

"I think I'll take a drive over to Slovenia while I'm here, but I'll use the official border crossing."

"I will take you. You may not take the rented car. The insurance, you understand?"

Libby hadn't read the fine print in her insurance policy, so she felt doubly grateful that she had someone like Vivia to explain things. She spent the next ten minutes trying to memorize the route they took to Cividale.

The grocery store looked fairly similar to those in Canada. This one had a flat front with a sixties-looking arch over the entrance where the word *Supermercado* was posted in huge letters. Rows of cars lined the large lot. When she opened the car door a blast of heat hit her. The temperature in the valley floor was much higher than up in the village. She followed Vivia to fetch a cart and was surprised to see them chained together in a metal corral. Vivia inserted a coin and tugged one of the carts free.

Inside the store, Vivia picked up a small basket and explained that she'd be back in a few minutes. Libby moved up and down the rows squinting at the Italian writing on boxes. Many of the brands were the same as those in Canada, with slight changes in the packaging. She bought cardboard cartons of milk that didn't appear to need refrigeration until opened. Unfortunately, she couldn't tell which were skim and which were whole milk, so, rather than wait to ask Vivia, she picked up one of each.

She rolled by the meat section ogling the posters of different cuts, including those of horse. The produce department was impressive. Since Vivia was nowhere in sight, Libby stood aside and watched how the other shoppers did things. People pulled on plastic gloves they fetched from baskets scattered here and there. Then they chose their type of fruit or vegetable, put the selection in a plastic bag, set it on a scale, and tapped in the number that hung above the bin of that product. A sticky label shot out of the machine. Efficient and clean.

By the time Vivia found her in the hardware section, Libby's basket overflowed with everything from mops to muffins.

"I am sorry to be slow," Vivia said. "I talked to a friend."

"Please don't be sorry. I'm grateful for your help. And I'm not in a hurry."

"You found what you want?" Vivia asked, peering into the cart. Her own basket held only some small tins and bread.

"Yes, I think so. I couldn't buy perishables because I don't have a fridge."

Vivia looked confused, then her face cleared. "*Frigorifero, sì.* You need the electricity."

They were headed toward the cashiers. "I can use a cooler for now, but it's soon going to be too hot for that."

"We go to the fridge store?"

"Oh, that would be lovely. If you have time? I don't want to inconvenience you."

Vivia linked her arm through Libby's. "Bah. It is nearby. And we will have fun, yes?"

After Libby and Vivia each paid for their groceries and loaded them into the trunk, they returned the empty cart to the corral. Then they walked around the corner to another large store with a display of striped sun umbrellas out front.

Once inside, Libby paused to get her bearings: house wares, clothing, toiletries, bedding, furniture. They wandered around for a couple of minutes, ending up in the large appliances section. Large, that is, by Italian standards. The washers and dryers, for example, weren't much bigger than apartment-size ones in Canada.

"They're so compact," she said to Vivia. "Perfect for Nonna. If only there were power."

"You may use my washer if you want."

"Thanks. I will, at least until I get things organized. Do you think the barn has electricity?" She meant the one attached to her house in the village.

"Yes. We, the men, use it, you know?" She frowned as if Libby might object to that.

"Nonna doesn't need a barn. I'm sure it's no problem. But if it has power already, that might make it easier to wire the house."

A young male clerk approached and, obviously having overheard their exchange, asked in excellent, if accented

English, "May I help you? You are looking for something?"

"Soon, when I have electricity." She ran her hand over the stainless top of a cook range.

He followed her gaze. "You don't need electricity for that."

"I don't?" She hitched her purse higher on her shoulder. "But . . . I don't know if there is a gas line to the house."

"You buy a tank and get it refilled."

"Like a barbecue tank?"

"Yes."

She perked up. "Show me what you have."

Twenty minutes later, with a new stainless-steel range jutting out of the trunk and the car's small rear seat filled with bags, Libby and Vivia motored back up the road toward Croce. With the extra weight, the car didn't have as much pep, but it obediently sped up the steep inclines and around the jagged turns.

"I will get Drago and my father. They will help you. There is a . . ." Vivia stopped, searching for the word. She released the wheel and made a motion as if grabbing onto something and pushing.

"A cart or wheelbarrow." Libby breathed again when Vivia grabbed the steering wheel.

"*Sì*. It is in the barn."

This time, when they passed the turnoff to the Iacome property, Libby paid more attention. Although the name of the estate wasn't written out, she saw a sign with a beautiful painting of grapes framed in woven vines.

"Is it true what Marc said about the families not getting along?" she asked.

Vivia gave a weary sigh. "It is true."

"But not everyone must feel that way? Do you?"

"Is *stupido*."

"I'm so glad to hear that," Libby said, thinking about how Marc and his cousin would be visiting her house the following morning. She was about to explain that when Vivia interrupted.

"But is true."

"True?"

"We do not, er, visit those people. They do not visit us. It is the way."

Libby scoffed. "In this day and age."

"Yes, in this day and age."

It was a few hours before Libby ventured down the mountain in search of Marc's aunt, this time the captain of her own ship. The trip took much longer to the Iacome winery since Libby felt obliged to keep her foot on the brake practically the whole way even though she drove in a low gear.

The approach to the Iacome winery was merely a widening in the road, but there she saw again the lovely painting of a cluster of purple grapes. She turned left onto a narrow, paved road where trees grew in a canopy overhead, making it feel like a dark tunnel. Finally, after zigzagging upward, she came to a fork. She braked and after a moment of trying to picture the map she'd studied, she turned to the right.

"Oh my," she said aloud, coming upon a three-story house that looked like an Austrian chalet. She mused that the style didn't seem out of place here on the side of a mountain. Besides, Austria and Italy shared a border only a couple of hours north of there.

Each level had its own exterior balcony with carved wooden banisters, large windows and, at the roof's peak, carved supports. The lower half of the house gleamed white stucco; the upper half was softened with a reddish wood. Judging by the piles of boulders and a partially completed wall, someone was building a terrace. Clearly she'd stumbled upon a private home and not the Iacome vineyard. She lingered there a moment admiring the structure, and then made a big turn in the driveway. Once she was headed in the other direction she realized that the view from there was every bit as spectacular as that from Nonna's balcony.

Retracing her route to the fork in the road, and this time choosing the opposite lane, there was no mistaking the Iacome business when she reached it. A manicured lawn led to a warehouse-size building. Below this spread countless rows of grape trellises. Above it were houses. Libby parked and approached a man working on a garden bed.

"*Mi scusi,*" she said, indicating the houses on the side of the slope. "*Dove* Marana Iacome?"

"*Sì.*" He pointed to the middle one.

Libby thanked the man, then drove over to Marana's house. It was a meticulous two stories with a flat front. Olive trees grew in the yard.

Marana, Marc's aunt, the woman she'd met briefly in the village, answered her knock, but the smile froze on her face when she recognized Libby.

Turning on her charm she said, "Hello. Remember me? Libby Zufferlia? We met?"

"Mattia Loszach's. Yes? What?" Marana lifted her shoulder in question but her eyes looked suspicious and unfriendly.

"I would like to rent your house in Croce."

Now Marana's head jerked back as though the very thought was incredible. "Not possible. Good-bye." She started to close the door.

"Please," Libby said, "can't we talk about this? It would only be for a couple of weeks. Marc said it's empty now."

"No. Is not possible."

"I will pay a fair rent—"

"Good-bye."

Libby gaped at the closed door for an instant, then she swung around and marched back to her own car. The woman was insufferably rude. Was it because when she arrived from the airport she'd mistaken her house for Nonna's? She did trespass, but not on purpose. That had all been explained. Or was it, as Marc had said, that Marana wouldn't rent to a Loszach? Incredible. Since when did someone turn away good money because of another person's ancestry? It was absolutely medieval. As she opened her car door, she glanced back at the house and saw Marana standing blatantly in the window, her arms crossed over her chest, watching her.

Libby smiled and waved, just to be contrary. As she drove back to the village, Libby wondered at how angry she felt. Her stomach clenched and she was playing little imaginary scenes in her head about how she'd get back at Marana. She shook her head. Is that how this so-called feud worked? An Iacome does something to hurt me so I do something to hurt her? Then she gets back at me and I get back at her? Those boys she'd seen fighting in the parking area. Was that an Iacome versus a Loszach incident?

In that light, the feud seemed horribly possible.

The next morning, Marc poked his head into Libby's kitchen. *"Permesso?"*

"Come in," she said. The rush of pleasure she felt at seeing him must have been obvious so she cleared her voice before asking nonchalantly, "Where's your cousin?"

"He'll be here soon."

The new stove stuck out like a shiny new thing amid a cluster of stone. "You have been busy."

"Would you like a cup of coffee?" she asked, feeling slightly smug at making the offer.

"Yes, thank you."

He went to the sink and washed his hands. "I fell," he explained at her startled look.

"Are you hurt?"

"No, just muddy." An oval of moisture stained one of his knees.

"I take it you came up over the embankment out back?" She tossed him a hand towel. "And this village is so full of well-used lanes and streets. Many lead right to my door. You should try one."

Sidestepping her obvious sarcasm, Marc continued, "It needs to be cleared of the bushes and trees."

"Why are you going through this trouble? This is borderline silly, Marc. I do have a front door." He concentrated on drying his hands and she met his silence with a sigh. "Well, I hope there's something I can do to repay you?" He leered at her, clearly teasing, so she rushed to add, "Or that you'll let me pay you for your time? In money," she added hastily as he wiggled his eyebrows. She found herself laughing.

He winked at her. "It's no problem. This is fun. A nice change."

"Did you do this all by yourself?" he asked, admiring he new stove, even leaning around to check the connection to the fuel tank.

"You don't need to sound so surprised," she teased. She went on to explain how it had taken some finagling. First, she and her cousin Vivia had tracked down her Uncle Victor, who had the key to the adjacent barn, so she could borrow the wheelbarrow. She had trundled all the groceries down to the house and gone back to the car. With Victor's help, they unloaded the stove and its parts, wheeled it down to the house, and set it up. Marc enjoyed her mime of the full and unsteady wheelbarrow.

"You know your family here in Italia?" he asked.

"I've only ever met them in person once before, but there have always been letters and phone calls to keep the family in touch."

"It was good of your uncle to help you with this."

Marc didn't look her in the eye as he said this. Libby wondered if she heard a grudging tone in his voice too.

"And then Uncle Victor and the whole crowd fed me," she continued. It had been a loud, enjoyable dinner at Victor's house with the whole Loszach clan, her extended family: Great Aunt Erika and her husband Naldo, Uncle Victor and Aunt Natale, Cousin Vivia, Cousin Drago with his wife Melena and their three children. "It went on all evening. They initiated me to the wonders of grappa." She rolled her eyes, remembering the courses upon courses of food and the strong drink.

He smiled knowingly. "How's your head?"

"I'm a little fuzzy this morning. Grappa packs a wallop."

"Packs a wallop. Interesting . . . I take your meaning though."

They enjoyed the moment before Marc's tone turned more serious. "Well, it seems you already have people to help you get this house fixed."

"Oh, no," she objected. "I have a lot of relatives who can bake breads and sweets, some who can do accounting and others who can run businesses, but, as you must know, none of them are tradesmen."

"No tradesmen?"

Was it the language difference that had him repeating the phrase? She decided to clarify. "Not a plumber, not a carpenter, not an electrician in the bunch."

Now Marc looked around the room. "You've done a lot of work in here."

The kitchen looked clean, but still tattered. "I want to make some pretty curtains. The old ones were only held together by dust and determination."

Marc slid out a chair and sat at the table. "You were going to fix me coffee?"

Suddenly, Libby felt acutely aware of him. The simple domestic scene triggered something deep within her. Marc, with his long legs and broad shoulders, was proportionally too large for the small furniture. He grinned at her as if he knew what was going through her head.

"Right." She poured the milk into a tall, narrow pot to heat it. "I hope this is the right kind of milk. I can't understand the carton," she said, passing it to him.

"Let's see. It is whole milk."

She scrunched down so she could adjust the flame under the pot of milk. He watched her, she knew, and it made every muscle in her body tingle.

"You went to see my aunt yesterday, about renting."

"She wouldn't discuss it."

"I'm sorry if she was abrupt, but I did warn you. She's actually a nice person . . . normally."

Libby considered Marana's behavior to be a little more extreme than abrupt. Rude would sum it up nicely. "I gather she hates me because of who my ancestors were?"

"Hate is a strong word," he replied, not really answering her question.

Tiny bubbles formed around the perimeter of the milk pot. When she dipped in the spoon and then held it to her tongue, it was barely warmed. She happened to glance at Marc at that moment, and he was watching her mouth with an absorbed expression.

"You're not abrupt with me," she said.

Libby fetched the big round cups from the cabinet and set them on the large saucers. Then she picked two spoons from the draining rack. Meanwhile, Marc pulled the milk off the burner, slipped the plunger into the pot, and thrust it up and down with slow even strokes. He poured the coffee and the foamy milk into the mugs at the same time. She liked that he made himself at home so easily; he didn't seem to be the kind of old-fashioned man who expected a woman to wait on him.

He took a sip of the coffee, then licked the arc of white foam off his upper lip, making an appreciative sound. Her mouth went dry at the sight, so she gulped her own coffee and had to restrain herself from sputtering. It was hot.

"Is the coffee okay?" she asked. "My cousin Vivia showed me how to make it."

He shifted his shoulders. "I'm used to stronger." When her face fell, he added, "We drink it stronger. But next time, I will show you."

Next time. "Okay."

A shadow passed the window over the sink, the one facing the alley that led to the back garden. "That must be your cousin."

Chapter Five

Libby's eyes scanned from face to face, exploring each feature for family similarities. Enzo and Marc shared the same amused brown eyes, but where Marc's met hers with direct humor, Enzo's looked down. Where Marc stood over six feet tall and defined the expression "broad-shouldered," Enzo was more Libby's height and gave life to the word *wiry*. Both men were good-looking. Marc was classically attractive while Enzo was handsome in the traditional sense. Both wore jeans with work gloves waving to her from back pockets, and lightweight jackets over T-shirts. Marc's hands rested with ease but Enzo's worked energetically at the hat he held. All in all a very pleasant sight.

"Please come in. You must be Enzo. I'm Libby. Thank you so much for coming." Reaching for Enzo's hand, she shook it with vigor and glanced back at Marc to encourage him to translate for her.

A rosy blush blossomed on Enzo's face. He looked young, but on closer inspection Libby was surprised that he was the older of the two. And very shy. How cute.

"I understand you're a carpenter?" She formed the statement as a question.

Marc patted Enzo's shoulder proudly. "He's a carpenter, electrician, and plumber."

"Then I'd say he's a gift from heaven."

"Perhaps, he doesn't have his . . . ah . . . official papers yet in all three trades exactly," Marc conceded, "but he's very good. And one day he will take over his father's contracting business. He knows the equipment, machinery." He paused to translate for his cousin. Enzo's face reddened even more.

The men spoke for a moment in Italian, then Marc turned to Libby. "I must watch the time. My crew will be wondering where I've gone."

"Let's do it then." Libby rubbed her hands together. "Come on in. I'll show you around the place first and point out what I'd like to accomplish."

The three of them toured the house, stopping here and there to take measurements. Soon, Enzo's notebook filled with drawings and numbers. He rarely looked Libby in the eye, but instead asked Marc the questions, which Marc then translated into English. Half an hour later, they ended up in the back garden, under the balcony.

The men studied the ground, the walls, talking, hands waving this way and that. As Libby couldn't follow the words, she inspected the overgrown garden. She could see some of the stonework now mostly covered with plants creeping through the patterns. The bones of the design remained in place. How'd she'd love the time to rejuvenate it. The dew in the tall grass had soaked through her sneakers, making her toes chilly. A giant black slug dragged itself along the top of the wall that protected the garden from the sudden drop into the woods below. She had never seen a slug so large so she leaned close to it and smiled when it lifted its snout and waved its head as if to warn her off.

Libby hoped that her grandmother would restore the garden. It wouldn't take too much work; it was smaller than her garden at home. She realized that the men had stopped talking.

"The cistern will go here," Marc translated. "He'll probably have to use a jackhammer to excavate."

"Are you saying that Enzo will take the job?" she asked, amazed. It was more than she'd hoped. "He can spare a month?"

"The timing is good for him. He's starting an apprentice position in six weeks."

"He hasn't apprenticed yet?"

"In carpentry and electrical. Now it's plumbing." Marc's pride in his friend was obvious. "And he learned at his father's knee. Don't worry; Iacomes are the best at what they do. And it was Enzo who did all the work on my aunt's house." Marc translated rapid-fire.

Excellent experience, she thought. *Perfetto.* "And what does he charge?"

Marc asked his cousin and reported. "He will charge you the same as he charged Aunt Marana."

"Speaking of your aunt, is that Enzo's mother?"

"Marana? No. His grandfather was my grandfather's cousin."

"How do you remember all those connections? You make my eyes cross it's so complicated."

A quick translation had the trio sharing laughter.

Libby fairly bounced ahead of them as they walked back toward the house. "And he won't mind people knowing where's he's working?"

Marc heaved an elaborate shrug as he turned to ask Enzo a question. They talked back and forth for a few minutes, then more pointing and hand motions ensued. Libby paced, waiting. What was Enzo's take on this whole Iacome and Loszach rift? He must know she was a descendent of "evil" Loszachs? Her stomach churned with a brief recognition of anxiety.

Finally, Marc returned. "We will not mention where he is working."

She flattened her palm against her chest. "How would that work?" Looking at Enzo she gestured with her hands. "How can you keep it a secret? You have to truck in heavy things, like bags of concrete and sinks and . . ."

"People are used to seeing him. He is my cousin and a good friend. Besides, he will come up that way." Marc pointed to a muddy track that led along the side of the garden and then, apparently, entered the woods.

Libby's head nodded back and forth between the men

as though watching a tennis match on fast-forward. It looked as if Enzo didn't think there was anything wrong with his sneaking in the back way.

"Libby, Enzo says he will prepare a list and that you can arrange for the materials to be delivered to your house."

"And Enzo's truck? Is he going to tote his tools through the forest?"

"He'll leave what he can each day. My house isn't far." He pointed down the slope. "He can park there."

Libby was about to throw out another concern when it occurred to her that she wasn't in any position to quibble. She needed the work done. If Enzo wanted to risk the wrath of the scary women in his family, what business was it of hers? If anything, she should feel gratitude toward the men.

Grinning, she grabbed Enzo's hand and shook it again enthusiastically. "You're hired. Thank you so much. Both of you. Thank you."

The next few days passed in a flurry. Libby spent much of her time driving up and down the mountain and, when she was at home, it was to wait for deliveries. A stream of men appeared at her door with carts of everything from boxes of tiles to power meters.

She and Enzo communicated patiently with hand signals and drawings, and every evening she sent him back to Marc's with a list of questions written in English. He returned the next morning with the answers and a list of questions of his own, which Marc had translated into English. The language difficulty aside, they worked well together whether it was with Libby holding the end of a board or Enzo holding a fixture steady while she pulled off the packing material.

It was a happy and productive time for Libby.

Early Friday evening, she stood before the wavy kitchen mirror trying to scrub paint off her face. Despite feeling physically tired, her body itched with restlessness. She considered dropping in on Cousin Vivia. Her kitchen table, she felt sure, would be draped in a pressed cloth, whereas planks of miscellaneous lengths of wood covered Libby's. Her home would be sparkly clean. Libby could write her name in drywall dust on the mirror she looked into. Vivia would have electric lights and something cold from the refrigerator, whereas she still used room-temperature milk from a carton.

She climbed the two flights of stairs to her top-floor room, the only spot in the whole house not currently under renovation. It had become a cozy refuge with a comfy four-poster and pretty new sheets. Each morning, when she sat up in bed, she looked out the window over the Natisone Valley, Cividale, and on clear days, the Adriatic. Even now, at the end of a long week, she took a moment to drink in the view as the sun dipped lower in the sky.

She'd been cooped up in the house all week. Her legs ached for a good long walk. Libby went back into her bedroom and pulled the walking stick from where she'd stored it in the wardrobe. The knobby wood felt smooth and strong in her hands. First thing tomorrow, she'd hike the mountain.

Tonight she would rest up, pamper herself with wine

and candles. After a trip down to dig in the dresser on the second floor for more candles, and another to the box currently acting as her pantry, she returned to set the stage. She hummed as she placed the candleholders in flat spots on the stones, lighting each one before moving on. A glorious sensation of contentment drifted with her blood through her veins. Here she was, in Italy, accomplishing wonderful things for her nonna, learning the language, and getting to know her roots. She had much to be proud of. Only one more thing could make her mood *perfetto*.

"Libby." Her imagination had taken full flight. She must be hearing things.

"Libby." She froze. Was that someone calling?

"Libbyyy."

Marc! With her heart racing, Libby scooted across to the edge of the balcony. Marc waved at her from the garden below. After motioning for him to come up, she jogged down the stairs and managed to unlock the gate at the bottom just as Marc reached it.

"Hi." She was breathless.

He had a dusky shadow of stubble on his face, and his nose and upper cheeks were tinged with sunburn. He was beautiful. He was there. It was with effort that she held herself from grabbing the front of his jacket with both hands, pulling him forward, and kissing those lips. He must have sensed her feelings because instead of making to step beside her, he leaned his face closer as if in invitation. She stood on tiptoe and let her mouth take over what her heart desired. Gently. She tasted him. Shyly. She tested his welcome. Her lips parted slowly.

She was dreaming. One moment she had been standing on her balcony as the sun set, and the next minute she was in Marc's arms, clutched there in his strong embrace. He smelled of earth and leaves.

She lowered herself from his mouth and stared up into his face. She had lost her mind, acting without thought that way, but it felt so right. So natural. So delicious. She wouldn't feel embarrassed. She couldn't.

He stared at her with a stunned but pleased look. After a moment he leaned back to pull the gate closed behind him. Then held up his package and said, "I brought an offering."

"Oh, come on up." Her voice sounded husky.

She led the way back up to the balcony, all the while conscious of him watching her from behind. They arrived at the top and he surveyed the candles, each casting its own magic. She remained silent.

He unpacked the bag he'd brought. A bottle and two glasses. "I hope it is not presumptuous." He opened the bottle with a practiced twist of his pocket corkscrew and poured them each some of the bloodred wine. She motioned to the marble benches along the wall. After waiting until she was comfortable, he sat close to her.

They sipped in the candlelight. The wine tasted glorious, so smooth she had to consciously keep herself from gulping.

"I'm glad you've come," she said softly. "I've been feeling a bit lonesome."

"Your family, they are not keeping you company?"

She shook her head. "No one besides Vivia has come

by. I told them I wanted them to see the house when it was finished, not the mess in the meantime. Thought that would be best, considering that Enzo doesn't want it widely known that he's working here."

He took a moment, as if digesting that information. "Good idea."

"It's such a beautiful evening." She forced lightness to her voice. She would deal with the kiss and what had possessed her later. He seemed happy to sidestep the whole event.

A slight rose fragrance drifted from the overgrown shrubs below. "Do you smell that? The roses? It must have been a beautiful terrace down there at one time. I hope I've got enough time to work down there, restore some of its beauty, before I have to go home again."

His eyes clouded briefly, then he rose and wandered to the end of the balcony. "You have a garden where you live?"

"It's very small," she said, joining him. "I own a condominium. It's stuffed with plants though. And the weather is more extreme there than it is here. I can't, for instance, grow olive trees like that one." She pointed below.

"It needs pruning."

She breathed in the crystal air, letting the evening coolness of it tingle her nostrils and fill her lungs. Although she'd only been here a short time, she noticed the days were getting warmer and longer. She sighed with pleasure.

"You like it here," Marc said softly.

"I do. It's not at all what I expected. I thought I'd feel all sorts of resentment, about Nonna moving here, about the family . . . tension." She moved away from the balcony and reached for her wine.

Once again, they sat together in the twilight.

"You know, when my grandmother told me she wanted to move here, I was shocked. I pictured this house, crude and backward. And the village." She shook her head at her own shallow assumptions. "But really, I think I was being selfish. I don't want her to be far away from me. She's a very special woman. A wonderful woman."

She glanced up at Marc but his face was blank, unreadable. "But Nonna insisted that she'd made up her mind."

Abruptly, Marc stared at her. "Did she say why she decided to come back?"

"Not really. I mean, I can guess. Now with Nonno gone, she probably wants to be with people who know where she came from. You know? Her family."

"But she has family there."

"Yes, but no one of her own generation." She shrugged her shoulders. "Anyway, I want her happy. Now that I'm here, I can see what she misses. Life moves more slowly up here, but it's just a quick trip down the mountain and there's all the benefits of modern living. Cities, art, shopping."

"You've hardly left the village; you've experienced so little of Italia."

"There'll be time for that." She gazed off into the distance. "What I've experienced I have loved."

Libby took a big breath. Should she ask Marc to go on

a trip with her? Away from the mountain and all the tensions of Iacome versus Loszach? He obviously liked her. And hadn't he already asked her if she wanted to hike on the mountain? She glanced back at the walking stick she'd left propped against the wall. What if he said no? It wasn't like her to dither like this.

Chapter Six

While the coffeepot heated on the propane stove, the battery lamp cast its feeble light, augmenting the orange light from the newly rising sun, and Libby bustled around the kitchen preparing her small backpack. She'd need a camera, water, sunglasses, a hat with a peak, and the nifty, old knobby walking stick.

Over her T-shirt, she wore a baggy sweatshirt that she could haul off and tie around her waist if she got too warm. What if it was really cold up on the mountaintop? Should she bring a vest? On the other hand, Vivia had advised her to go early in the morning and avoid the heat of the day.

She opened the kitchen door and, arms crossed around her middle, stepped out onto the street. Croce slept still, but the sky to the east shimmered with the promise of a clear day. A cow's bell clanged melodiously in a nearby field, but all else remained silent. The buildings across the street, already whitening from their predawn blue, hid the view of the mountain that loomed over the village, but it waited there. She intended to make it to the top.

A scraping sound down the street had her tensing. Then a dog emerged from the shadows. Libby relaxed. She knew this little fella; he belonged to the elderly couple who usually sat on kitchen chairs outside their house. She ran a hand over the old dog's head as she remembered when, a couple of days earlier, the elderly lady had given Libby a toothless smile and asked a question. The phrase sounded familiar, so Libby had answered that yes, it was a beautiful day. The woman looked startled. Then Libby realized the question had been "What is your name?"

The memory had her cringing in embarrassment.

After that, Libby pushed herself to learn more Italian. There was no peace for poor Enzo. She started by waving a broom saying, "Broom! Broom!" Enzo, scarlet faced, stared at her. She felt sure he wished she'd fly away on it. She grabbed the chair. He flinched. "Chair. Chair." Her voice seemed to grow louder with every attempt to be understood. "Bowl!" she'd yelled, holding it toward him like a demented version of Oliver Twist. And then the light went on inside his head. She could see it.

It turned out that Enzo knew more English than she had first assumed. It was his shyness that kept him from speaking it. "Bowl," he'd said, "*Scodella*. Broom. *Scopa*. Chair. *Sedia*." And on it went.

She smiled at the memory. She and Enzo had had some laughs during the lessons. Now she went back into the house to toast bread over the flames of the stove.

By the time Libby parked in the lot at the base of the trail to the top of the mountain, the sun had risen fully. She hoisted on the backpack, snugged on her cap, and grabbed the walking stick firmly in her grasp. She felt relieved to see a couple moving up the incline only a few minutes ahead. She wouldn't have to wait for companion hikers.

She fixed a bead up there on her goal. Oh, but it was impossibly steep and so far to the tiny church that now looked like a miniature at the top of the mountain. She took a deep breath and started to climb.

Marc tossed a thermos and paper bag of crème-filled buns next to the water carrier and binoculars already on his truck's seat. It was far too early to be heading up, he guessed, but what difference did it make? He would wait for her. And if she didn't show and he ended up having a picnic breakfast by himself, the trip would still be worthwhile. And what a great day to enjoy the view.

He hoped she'd show. The day before, Enzo had mentioned a conversation he'd overheard between Libby and her cousin, and thought it had to do with a hike up the mountain early in the morning. He said she had shown Vivia an old walking stick.

Marc rolled down the window, started the engine and, as he tooled his way up the twisty road, whistled a melody that he couldn't name but sounded catchy to his ear.

Would Libby smile when she saw him, and look surprised? Of course she would. She always smiled. She had a great smile. She'd ask him what brought him to the hiking trail this early in the morning. He pondered that thought for a moment. Why did he set his alarm and go to all this trouble when he could have been sleeping in, or working on his conservatory? Why not? It might be fun, and he always welcomed a change to his routine. And he might get to kiss her again. All the while he rationalized this to himself, a niggle of guilt fought to surface.

The previous day when his mother had interrogated him about what he had learned from Libby about why she was restoring the house, he had to admit that he hadn't really known. Now he did. Now he knew that Mattia Loszach planned to move back to Croce. He hoped he wouldn't run into his mother or aunt for a while. He'd have to make his report. Then they'd announce that their worst fears had been realized. No doubt they would nag him to stop seeing Libby. He didn't want to stop seeing her.

What harm would it do? She'd be gone in a couple of months. What his mother didn't know couldn't hurt her.

Marc fully expected to sit on one of the stone walls and have his breakfast while he waited to see if Libby would come, but a number of cars already sat in the parking area. He slipped out his binoculars and focused on the people above on the mountainside, working their way up the zigzagging trail. One figure stood out.

"Well, well . . . Libby Zufferlia! You rose early." He liked that in a woman. It showed she had energy, and an energetic woman was usually an enjoyable one. She certainly was.

He grabbed his satchel and, eschewing the easier grades of the trail, leaped over boulders and banks to catch up. Five minutes later, when he was within yards of Libby, he saw her lean over from the waist as if she were catching her breath. He held back so as not to embarrass her.

"Libby," he called when he deemed she'd had enough time to catch her breath.

She swung around. "Marc?"

"May I join you?"

She hesitated. "Ah . . . what are you . . . that is . . ." She grimaced. "This is a coincidence."

He shrugged, not willing to tell her he'd come because of her, or give himself away just yet.

"You don't want to join me, Marc. I'll just hold you back."

Her cheeks were rosy, and a flush crept up her throat. He'd embarrassed her. "I'm not in a rush, Libby, but if you'd rather walk alone, I understand. First, will you join me for some coffee and a snack? There's a flat spot a little farther on."

A water bottle hung from a lanyard around her neck. She took a drink before answering. "Is it okay to eat when you're hiking?"

"A little snack won't hurt you. Please?"

"Well then, that sounds lovely. Thank you."

Marc led Libby off the main track. They chatted about the view as they worked their way around a couple of stony outcroppings to a clearing alive with wildflowers.

"Oh," she said with a sigh. "This is lovely."

She dropped down onto her knees and ran her fingers over a mound of purple blossoms. "Look at that. Bell-flowers growing wild. And primrose. And look, those are pincushion flowers. But they're all so tiny." Her face glowed. "Are there any edelweiss?"

Marc had been so captivated by the sight of Libby there amid the flowers that it took a moment for him to replay her question in his mind before he could answer. "I don't see any. They are the fuzzy white ones, yes?"

"I think so. I've only ever seen them in pictures. But this is an alpine meadow, so I'm guessing they grow here. Are these little lady-slipper ones some kind of orchid?"

He laughed. "You ask me? I am not a flower kind of man. Give me trees, big trees." He slapped his chest, then raised a finger. "But my mother would know."

"She's a gardener?"

He chuckled. "She would garden always, if she could."

Libby sat with her legs stretched out before her, and rested back on her elbows. "Does she work? You know, at a job outside the home?"

He sat beside her. "She is an accountant for the winery. The boss in the office. She is very good."

"Oh, the same as Vivia."

"No," Marc said, "not the same."

Her eyebrows lifted as if she waited for him to continue, but he remained silent so she asked, "Is that how she met your father? At work?"

He shook his head. "They met in the vineyard. He's gone now. He died several years ago."

"I'm sorry."

He pulled the bag closer, flipped over the canvas flap, and pulled out a tea towel. As he unrolled the two ceramic mugs from the linen, he caught Libby's eye. She looked amused.

"Your mother, Vivia, and I have a lot in common," she ventured. "I garden a bit, Viv's an accountant too, and I have accounting training, though I'm not certified yet. I think I'd like your mother."

He was careful not to answer as he poured the coffee. Libby might like his mother, but his mother would never allow herself to like Libby.

"You don't mind that I joined you?" he asked.

She took her coffee with a smile. "No, this is nice."

"If you had a mobile phone, I would have called you first."

"This early? If I hadn't been coming on the hike, I'd still be asleep. But you're right. I should have a cell. Enzo seems to think I'm backward because I don't have one yet."

A notion suddenly occurred to him. "I'll help you buy it."

"I'd appreciate that very much."

"Would you like to go to Venice with me on Monday? We can pick up the phone while we're out."

She gaped at him. "Venice?"

Oh, he'd love to show her the city, its heart, its essence. "I know you need to work on the house. And it is a long drive; we would have to be gone all day. But I think you would like it there."

He'd asked on an impulse but the idea appealed to him more and more. He loved to share his country with others. And what harm could it do to take a Loszach for a drive? His family need never know. It occurred to him that he was justifying his own pleasure, even taking a day off work to do so. Then he wondered at why he had to justify it. This antipathy between the families shouldn't have anything to do with him, with the people he chose to see. As long as it didn't hurt his loved ones at home, that is. And he'd been working hard. He deserved a day off.

Libby's eyes glowed wide. "I've read about Venice my whole life. I've been dying to go." Her shoulders scrunched up toward her ears in excitement.

He had to grin at her. "We'll ride in a gondola and eat in a nice restaurant."

"I'll bring my camera. I can't believe it. I'm going to Venice."

She looked spectacular sitting there in the flowers. Like a Matisse painting. "Have you taken your camera with you today?"

She nodded and passed it to him without question. He examined it, turned it on, and held it up so he could look at her though the display window on the back. He zoomed in closer. She was flushed, her complexion brightened by the exercise and, he suspected, by the anticipation of her trip. Her dark hair was pushed back as she strove to cool herself. It startled him to realize that she was one of the most beautiful women he'd ever seen. Perhaps embarrassed by his scrutiny, she frowned and pulled a corner of her bottom lip between her teeth. Such a pretty bottom lip.

"Are you married?" she asked suddenly. "Do you have a girlfriend?"

He threw back his head and laughed.

Libby chuckled, saying, "I guess that means no."

"No girlfriend," he said, nodding. "No wife." A sudden thought had his stomach tightening. "Do you have a boyfriend? A husband?"

How had he never asked her that before? What if she said yes?

"No and no."

Relieved but a bit chagrined at his train of thought, he lifted the camera again. "Good."

Click. He caught her smiling right at the lens. He moved for a better angle. *Click.* Now she blushed. *Click.* Now she laughed, that lovely familiar sound. *Click.*

Now she was making threatening noises. "Okay, okay. My turn. Let's see how you like it." Libby grabbed the camera and turned it on him like a weapon. He mugged. He raised his arms over his head, like a fashion model. He licked his lips. All the while she *click, click, clicked.*

"Does this have a timer?" Marc moved toward her, pointing at the camera questioningly.

She nodded, catching his meaning. "I'll set it for multiple shots."

It took a moment to find the perfect spot, but with the camera set up and perched on an outcropping, they moved in close. His arm around her, they smiled at the camera. *Click.* His arm still around her they turned to face each other, smiling. *Click.* Holding that pose, he moved in closer and kissed her sweet lips. *Click.* And then to end the series, they chose an age-old tradition: They stuck out their tongues. *Click.*

Laughing, Libby reclined in the flowers. Her expression became dreamy. "Oh, look at the sky."

Marc lay so their sides touched. Downy white clouds suspended in a startlingly blue sky. It was pretty, yes, but nothing compared to the view beside him. He propped himself on an elbow and studied Libby. She inhaled and released a deep, contented sigh. "You are so beautiful."

She smiled up at him. "And you are so handsome."

He placed his palm on her face to smooth her hair from her soft cheek. She guided his hand to her mouth and, with her eyes still on his, nibbled the sensitive skin on the inside of his wrist. A sound, like a growl, came unbidden from deep within his throat. Then, very slowly, he lowered his lips to within a breath of hers. He held there, suspended by desire. Her eyes fluttered closed in anticipation and lifting her chin slightly, she captured his mouth.

Pleasure infused him. He moved closer still, scooping the length of her to him. His heart pounded. A flicker of flame licked his back as her fingers moved down his spine. Her hand splayed, pressing, telling him she felt the same. He buried his face in the soft, sweet-smelling crook of her throat and tasted.

"Marc," she whispered.

He forced himself to look at her. "Libby?"

"Listen." She lifted her shoulders from the ground. Her breath was jagged, but again she managed, "Listen."

Marc was confused. Listen? What was she saying? Again, her body struggled farther out of his embrace as she sat. She had his attention now. He listened.

It was the sound of people approaching. A high-pitched voice of a child, followed by the lower one of a man, talking. As much as he wanted to kiss Libby right then, right now, he wouldn't risk being discovered by a child.

They pulled apart, straightening their clothes, catching their breaths. At first he felt cheated, then he saw Libby's face. She grinned like a little, guilty kid. Laughing, he picked a bruised flower from her hair.

Libby could hardly believe how she was ready to kiss this man, right there on the mountainside. She was a sensual, modern woman, but to lose all sense like that and only a few short paces from a public path! What was she thinking? It made her smile all the more. She stood, reached for his hand, and helped him to his feet. Giggling, they packed up the picnic.

Forty minutes later, winded and hot, Libby boosted

herself over the last ledge and onto the top of Montagna Croce. She looked back at the way they'd come. A brown path wound its way through a green field, twisting here and there to skirt the many white mounds of bare rock. There would be other people down there, she knew, but she couldn't see them because of the way the path ended where the mountain dropped to another level. Marc helped her to her feet. She smiled at him and then saw beyond his shoulder.

"Oh." She sighed.

Behind them were rolling hills, each dimming to a grayer green as the distance increased, and spotted with occasional splashes of orange where the rooftops of villages poked up. Beautiful. But the view ahead was stupendous. The Julian Alps, real mountain peaks stabbing the sky, their tops white with snow and ice. She stared for a full five minutes, with her heart in her throat, before taking the time to look around the mountaintop.

A church, the building she'd seen as a tiny dot from below, turned out to be a symbol, more or less, not an operating church. It sat in the middle of the smooth mound of bare stone. The cement walls had been whitewashed, and weathered metal clad the roof. A large iron cross looked black against the blue of the sky.

A cool wind soon dried the moisture on Libby's skin, making her feel chilled, so she untied her sweatshirt from her waist and pulled it over her head. Marc took her hand and led her to a boulder where they could sit comfortably, safely, and still have a panorama to enjoy.

"Where does Slovenia start?" she asked.

"We're probably in Slovenia."

A river flowed in a cleft miles below their feet: a thin line of blue water, green hills on either side, then the gray-blue stone of the mountains.

"I didn't realize it was so close. I mean, I just walked to Slovenia." She shook her head in wonder.

"The border has changed back and forth over these mountains many times."

She glanced at his handsome profile and admired the way the wind waved through his hair. "You said the Loszachs were Slovenian."

"Have you not noticed the language in the village?"

"Their accent is different?"

"Many of the people, the older ones, don't even speak Italian." He frowned and shook his head as if displeased.

"Oh, is that why sometimes I can't even understand a single word when I hear people walking by. I thought I'd picked up quite a bit of Italian by now. So the village used to be in Slovenia?"

"Yugoslavia, more or less. The names and borders changed with every war." He pointed to the left. "That's Austria over there." His arm moved in an arc. "Slovenia in front of us, Croatia down to the south."

"It wasn't so long ago that Yugoslavia divided," she remembered. "Croatia, Slovenia, and Serbia. So the old people, they were born Yugoslavian?"

"They considered themselves Slovenian." He hooted a derisive scoff. "Your people still do."

She felt stung. "My relatives are Italian."

"Not really."

That wasn't the impression that her cousins gave her. She felt defensive. "The young people grew up as Italians and seem proud of it."

Marc gave her a disapproving look and seemed to be about to say something, but thought better of it. He reached for his water bottle and took a long drink.

Chapter Seven

Back home, when Libby was packing for this trip, she had considered her church clothing carefully. Her nonna always wore a dark dress and a hat when she went to mass. Was that because people in Italy did, or because she had done so in her youth? Libby settled on a pretty dress and a jacket that matched one of the colors in the pattern. In lieu of a hat, she tied a scarf around her neck. It could go on her head if the people in Croce were still formal when dressing for church.

Now, as she and Viv joined the people milling outside the church entrance, she realized she shouldn't have worried. No one wore shabby clothing like jeans, but few were dressed to the nines either.

Vivia introduced her to what felt like a crowd of new people, most of whom, she explained, only spent the weekends in Croce. They lived and worked down below in cities like Udine.

When a long, dark car pulled up, there was a slight change to the tone of voices, a few covert glances toward the street. Libby was deep in conversation with one of the women she'd just met so she glanced around only long enough to assure herself that Marc hadn't arrived. The impression she gleaned from that quick look was that of two proud-looking people, both well dressed, obviously wealthy.

When the time arrived to go inside, Libby allowed Vivia to guide her to a seat. She smiled at and nodded to many familiar faces, mostly of her own family members. It was only as the mass began that she realized that Marc had already arrived. He shared a pew a few rows ahead and on the other side of the church with the wealthy-looking people she'd seen arrive. She watched him, willing him to look around so she could catch his eye. He didn't.

Vivia leaned forward and whispered, "The Iacome people sit there."

Libby hissed to her cousin, "The church is segregated?"

Viv nodded complacently. "It is the way." Iacome there. Loszach here.

On Monday morning, Libby paced her balcony and sipped her orange juice. She wore comfortable clothing—her capris, a tank top, and her standby sandals, as easy on the feet as any walking shoes. She had stuffed a lightweight hoodie into her carryall with her camera and wallet. Just thinking about the camera made her smile.

When she caught a glimpse of color coming up through the trees below, she grabbed her shoulder bag and straw hat and jogged down the stairs. They met at the end of the garden.

Marc clutched her hand to steady her while she made her way down the slippery incline where Enzo had cleared a path. They emerged on a well-worn woods track. Here and there, the beaten-down earth circled around boulders and roots smoothed by years of feet. Above, the new leaves met in a green ceiling. When he didn't immediately release her hand, Libby risked looking at Marc's face. He bounced one eyebrow as if daring her to try to get her hand back.

"That way leads to the vineyard."

"Ah," Libby said with a nod. "It surprised me when I couldn't see any road between the vineyard and the village on my map. It was as if there were two different communities. That they could have been miles apart."

Libby felt, rather than saw, Marc tense, but he said nothing. It was a good opportunity, she knew, to get him to talk about their families' animosity. And she even formed the first question in her mind, but he distracted her with plans for the day. How could she dispel his buoyant mood with what really should have been ancient history?

Croce, 1947

The path felt different to Mattia Loszach today: softer underfoot, sweeter smelling, prettier looking.

She couldn't understand it. She and her friends had run and hid and played in these woods her whole life. She glimpsed the fairy rock through the new leaves. That's where she had believed, until not long ago, fairies lived. And why wouldn't they live there? It cried for them: a dark-green pool lined with moss-covered rocks where frogs and salamanders darted in and out of the shadows and crevices. Such a magic place. You could stick a pole down into the depths and never reach bottom; not that they'd ever tested that theory.

Today her heart sang. Today Leo Iacome waited for her in their secret spot.

She scampered down the incline until she neared the turnoff. Then she slowed her step and listened. Birds twittered. High above in the chestnut trees a breeze swished the leaves. She peered back up the path, then down. Alone. With a thrill of anticipation, she darted under a low branch and scrambled up an incline. Branches crackled underfoot. Finally, she reached the ledge. A strong hand reached over the edge of the rock. She looked up into Leo's handsome face, then gripped his hand and let him haul her the last few feet.

"Mattia," he whispered.

His look left her breathless and slightly shy. But she collected herself. "I came as soon as I saw the rope. Have you been here long?"

A dead branch, white and smooth, hung at the edge of the common field bordering Croce. Except for the handful of times a year when the field hosted a flea market, bonfire, or other celebration, only cows kept the grass sheared. It was a spot visible from the road but rarely used by people. If one of them wanted to see the other, he or she slung an old length of thick rope over the branch. No one knew about the signal, not even Mattia's best friend, Sophia.

"I don't mind waiting."

Leo had brought a blanket this time. He folded it onto a long rectangle so they could sit on the rock in comfort. Mattia knew the view was stupendous from there, but she only had eyes for Leo.

"I hope you don't mind," he said, taking her hand. "I only wanted to see you."

"And I wanted to see you." She smiled. "That's reason enough, don't you think?"

"*Cara.*" He kissed her fingers one after the other. She sighed at the sweetness. She was a woman now, sixteen, but Leo never pressed her for more than kisses. Even those, she knew, would horrify her parents and everyone else in the village. In Leo's as well.

As they had done dozens of times in the past, Leo and Mattia spent their stolen hour together in soft whispers and kisses. Promises were exchanged. Someday they would marry, despite the hatred between the two families. But not yet.

As usual, Mattia crept from their meeting place first. When she reached the main path, she pushed the branches aside and stepped through. Her heart jumped to her throat when she realized she wasn't alone.

Deborah, one of the girls from the enclave of people

belonging to the vineyard, was standing there as if she'd been waiting. Her fists braced on her thin hips, her face wild with anger.

Mattia hesitated for only a moment, debating what she should do, what she should say. Was Deborah there because she'd seen Leo go up the secret path? Or did she just happen to come along just now? She and Deborah had a long history of antipathy toward each other. There was a time back in grade school where the teacher had seated them both together. Mattia had tried to befriend Deborah but was met with nothing but haughtiness. Deborah was a pretty enough girl but not very popular. Mattia always suspected that she envied her big circle of friends and family.

Leo would soon be coming behind her so Mattia, anxious not to be there at the same moment, only nodded a greeting at Deborah. Then she quickly trod up the path toward Croce.

Croce, present day

Libby took a deep, cleansing breath of the mountain air. She had to savor this moment. What could be more perfect? She was walking along a lovely mountain track holding hands with a gorgeous Italian man who would be, this very day, driving her to Venice.

"How long a drive is it?" She couldn't stop smiling.

"Less than an hour, if we take the autostrada. Or would you like to see some of the countryside?"

"Not today. I want as much time as possible in Venice.

I know I'll probably go there again, but they say you can't see it in one day."

He looked pleased at her excitement. "That's true. I've been there a hundred times and I see something new every time."

"I'm so glad. I was afraid you'd be bored."

"No. I love the city. Not everyone does, you understand. There are many, many tourists. You must accept that as part of the charm."

"Is it your favorite Italian city?"

He pursed his lips, thinking. "I have many favorites. I love Firenze for the art, Roma for the nightlife, Milano for the beautiful women."

"Firenze is Florence in English?" she clarified.

"*Sì*. And Venezia is Venice."

"I don't know why we English-speaking people don't just use the real names."

Now they veered off to a newer path rough with boulders and tree roots. The smell of newly cut wood perfumed the air.

"I hope you like my house," Marc said. "I haven't finished the landscaping yet. Maybe you could help me with it?"

"I'd like that." In fact, she'd love that. Not only did she enjoy gardening, but also she felt she owed him so much for all the help he'd already given to her.

"Not with the work. With the ideas."

"I like getting my hands in the soil."

She judged, by the angle of their descent, that they were not going to the open terraces above the vineyard where his Aunt Marana lived. Could he own that beautiful Austrian-looking place she'd admired before? Finally, they stepped out into a clearing.

"I saw this house the other day," she cried. She jogged around to the other side with him in tow. "It's just gorgeous! You own this?"

"You like it?"

"I love it. Look at the carving up there."

"It adds something, don't you think? I didn't do it myself. I hired a man."

"What huge windows. And that stone wall . . . is there a massive fireplace behind there? Oh, Marc," she said on a sigh, "you must be so pleased with it."

"I am. I like it very much. My mother says it needs a woman's touch. It's very simple inside still. Maybe you can give me some advice?"

"I'd like that."

"But not today, I think. My car is over there."

Libby froze. "Is that your car? Is that a . . . Ferrari?" She hadn't really thought about what kind of automobile Marc drove, but this surprised her. He was usually so casual with his scruffy sneakers and faded jeans. But today he had on light-colored cotton slacks and a linen shirt that opened just enough at the neck that she spied a hint of curly chest hair.

"It's not new." He gave her a sidelong look. "I usually use that." He motioned toward a typical European workman's truck.

"Wow. Am I going to get to drive in a Ferrari?"

Now he grinned. "Come."

The trip to Mestre, the jump-off point to the islands that made up the city of Venice, went quickly. Marc drove the same speed as most of the other motorists on the highway, a dizzying 90 miles an hour. He darted in and out between cars and massive, blunt-ended trucks with ease, all the while talking like a typical Italian, with both hands. Libby enjoyed watching him, his tanned fingers adjusting the wheel, his eyes glancing into the rearview mirror, his obvious pleasure at the whole experience.

They parked in a multistoried complex and walked to the dock where Marc arranged for a private water taxi. Across green-blue water, the domes, steeples, and elaborate facades of Venice glowed in the sunlight. A gondola glided past. Libby felt as if she were watching a live fairy tale. The gondolier stood at one end of the craft, his feet actually riding with air between the boat's hull and the water because of its curved build.

Marc must have seen her keen interest. "It is too choppy out here for a gondola," he explained.

She grabbed his hand. "I've never even seen one before."

They settled onto the cushioned bench in the back of the speedboat and Marc nestled Libby snugly to his side. The driver cut away from the dock, veered toward the deep water, and opened up the throttle. Libby laughed aloud as a cool spray spattered her cheek.

"We'll go up the Grand Canal and around to St. Mark's Square. That's not my favorite part of Venezia, but everyone must experience it."

Libby was just happy to let him be the tour guide. She

gaped at the buildings lining the canals, their doors opening right onto the water. The arched, Moorish, or simple
square windows were like portals to an exotic land. Marc
said something to the driver and he slowed. They passed
gondolas carrying camera-snapping tourists, barges
heaped with paper or produce, and squat, ferry-shaped
boats that Marc explained were called *vaporettos*, or water busses. The Grand Canal, like the major thoroughfare
of any large city, curved through the city's waterways to
the other side of this, the largest of the Venetian islands.

The taxi let them off at a dockside. They joined the
crowds that funneled through the opening to the vast
paved area of St. Mark's Square.

They stood in the very middle of the square, in front
of the elaborate, frescoed beauty of the basilica. Libby
gaped at the ornate arches, statues and carvings, and
craned her neck to see the top of the bell tower. "It's
gorgeous, Marc. But almost too much."

"It is," he agreed as he shifted to protect her from a
pushy tour group. "This is the most famous place in
Venice, but not the most beautiful."

After the quiet of the village, the crowds of tourists,
hawkers selling masks and plastic gondolas, and the bar-
rage of intricate architecture did feel overwhelming. "I
wish I could come here when there were fewer people."

"Come in the winter. It is cold, but you can really see
the beauty, the architecture, the art."

In the winter. Libby tried to picture herself coming
back to Italy then. Perhaps she would, to visit her nonna.
And Marc. The thought of being away from this man had

Libby wrapping her arms around him and hugging possessively. He returned her hug.

With her cheek pressed against his chest, she eyed the arches in the five-story building running along one side of the square and wondered if it was it possible that people lived there. How proud they must feel to be a part of this unique city. Like living inside a gorgeous sculpture.

"Shall we move on?" he asked.

"Yes, please lead the way."

They walked beneath one of the arches that ran right through a building and emerged on a street that rose in a slight incline up to a bridge. A gondola passed below. She peered over the side and down into it to admire its red floor and ornately painted gold ornamentation. As they strolled away from the water, past awning-covered shops and businesses, the air grew warmer.

An hour later, Marc guided Libby down a narrow alley between two buildings. "We will go this way. It is shorter."

"I never would have considered taking this path. It's so . . . mysterious." She could picture seventeenth-century assassins lurking around the corners, their long capes swishing about their calves.

They emerged at the edge of the Grand Canal. The water lapped at the red-and-white painted wooden posts where gondolas were tied. Enjoying the breeze, they strolled, only stopping to listen to the musicians who played on the Rialto Bridge.

Libby felt tired and weak-kneed and they'd barely even seen any of Venice. "It's all so beautiful," she said, turning in a slow circle. Every direction had breathtaking architecture. "It's exhausting. Could we sit down for a moment? Have something cool to drink?"

"Lunch," he stated.

She'd assumed he'd lead her to one of the restaurants in sight, their tables and chairs spreading into a square. Instead, he wrapped her hand around his strong forearm and walked her through an arch to a narrow *via* beyond. There were shops on either side, with purses and hats, shawls and tourist knickknacks. They rounded half a dozen corners and crossed footbridges until Libby totally lost her bearings. There were fewer shops here, and those consisted of small groceries, a wine store, a window full of blocks of cheese.

"It will be quieter here," he explained.

And romantic, Libby thought as they entered a hushed café with linen-covered tables emerging on a balcony hanging over a narrow canal. Marc chatted with the waiter in Italian as if they were old friends.

"You must be a regular?" Libby asked after the man left. Or maybe Marc's ready charm just made everyone seem like his friend.

He shrugged. "Once a year perhaps. I asked him to bring us some menus and coffee, plus water. Is that okay?"

"Sounds wonderful."

They'd selected a table close to the canal. She'd heard that Venice was polluted, but it seemed very clean and tidy to her. The air smelled slightly briny. The building across the way had a flat facade and yet it was anything but boring architecturally. The lower floor, like all the other buildings lining the water, looked utilitarian, just a place to park the boat or unload groceries. The upper floors had high windows with curved tops. An iron balcony jutted from one. She imagined what that balcony must have witnessed over the centuries.

When the waiter returned, Libby realized Marc was smiling at her. "What?"

"I love watching you."

She chuckled. "I have been gaping, haven't I?"

"It's very appealing."

He reached across the round table, picked up her hand, and turned it over. He smoothed her fingers straight, running his thumb over her pulse point. With his eyes on hers, he bent his head and kissed her wrist. Libby almost whimpered as sensations traveled through her arm and landed deep inside her. What was it about him that made her feel this way? His shiny, tousled hair? His expressive eyes? Molded cheeks? Broad shoulders? Kissable chin? Or his luscious accent? Yes. All of that and something more. She reached for the ice water and took a large gulp.

When the waiter returned, he had the menus and a platter of prosciutto wrapped around melon slices. The sweet taste of the fruit married deliciously with the saltiness of the ham. Libby asked Marc to order a traditional Venetian meal for her, and he gave the matter his serious attention. A thick soup of beans and pasta was followed by a smoky-tasting grilled fish nestled on a bed of polenta, the cornmeal dish soft and smooth. In Italian fashion a salad of radicchio and artichokes appeared, accompanied by small bottles of balsamic vinegar and a green-tinged olive oil, followed the main course. The lemon sorbet drizzled with liquor was the perfect end. It took more than an hour for them to work their way through the various courses.

As they ate, Libby asked Marc about life in Venice, a city without cars, a city reportedly sinking into the ocean. He described things with his hands, the tilt of his head, his eyes, as well as with words. Clearly, he loved Venice and understood the tourists' fascination.

Then a tiny bird landed on the table and pecked at some crumbs beside the bread platter. Both Libby and Marc stilled, watching it. Suddenly the bird looked up, first cocking its head toward Libby, and then Marc. It was as if it suddenly realized it wasn't alone. In an ungainly flurry of wings, it lifted itself away.

Delighted, the two of them put their heads back and laughed.

They often laughed together, their senses of humor meshing. They never ran out of things to say. Libby realized she could talk with him all day and never grow bored.

Marc set his linen napkin aside. "Where would you like to go next? There are museums, art galleries?"

"Actually, I think I'd like to see some of the real Venice. The places were people live and shop. But first I need to digest some of this wonderful meal."

"You enjoyed it?" He looked pleased.

She rolled her eyes skyward. "It may have been the best meal I've ever eaten."

He picked up her hand and smoothed his long fingers over her knuckles. His voice was husky and full of meaning. "There are so many things I want you to experience, Libby."

Her voice deepened. "And I plan to enjoy every moment, Marc."

After the whirlwind tour of the city, they made their way back to the parking center and started toward home. Marc glanced at the clock on the dashboard. "The tobacco shop will still be open, but only barely."

"Tobacco shop?" Sated by the day's experiences, she'd been lolling against the leather car seat, content.

"For your mobile."

"We don't have to do it today."

He scoffed. "I do, or Enzo will cut my heart out."

"If you don't mind, then." Enzo, the house's renovations—she hadn't given them a moment's thought all day. Settling in for the drive, she slipped out of her sandals, set her car seat to its most reclined position, and allowed the motion to lull her.

When they reached Cividale, Marc parked the car next to the railroad station and they walked the few short blocks to where a statue of Julius Caesar, the town's founder, stood atop a white pillar. Libby had been admiring the way the cobbles on the street had been placed in a pretty scalloped pattern when she felt Marc's hand tighten in hers. She glanced up at him, but his face was pointedly expressionless.

They entered a small shop and waited quietly until the proprietor finished dealing with another customer. Then Marc and the man chatted in Italian, only occasionally translating for Libby's benefit. The deal was made. She paid for the purchase with euros, accepted the paper bag of goodies, and turned to leave.

There was her cousin, Drago Kidric. Pleasure had her smiling broadly as she approached him. "What a small world." He didn't return her smile. Apparently, he hadn't recognized the phrase so familiar to English-speaking people.

She started again, "Drago—what a wonderful time I have just had in Venice."

Although Libby had only met Drago at the family dinner a few days earlier, she had known his face all her life through snapshots Nonna received regularly. This was not the same face that had smiled into the camera.

Shifting to include Marc, she ventured, "You know Marcello Iacome. Marc, say hello to my cousin Drago."

"Drago," Marc said in an unfamiliar growl. His eyebrows lowered and a muscle twitched in his cheek.

Animosity sparked between the men. "So . . . ," she started, confusion creeping up her spine. "How are you?"

Drago uncrossed his arms, but he didn't take his eyes off Marc. "I am fine."

"And Melena? And the children?" Drago and Melena had three children, two little girls and a preteen boy.

Now he looked at her. "They are fine."

"Well, say hello to them for me, please."

He nodded. "What do you do here, Cousin Libby?" There seemed to be an exaggerated emphasis on the word *cousin*. "And why are you with this Iacome?"

This Iacome? Was he joking? "We've been to—"

Marc interrupted her. "You don't have to explain your business here in Cividale."

To Drago he said, "She needed help with the language to purchase a telephone. I was raised properly. I help when it is needed."

With his eyes now in mere slits, Drago addressed Libby, ignoring Marc's response. "You will come to eat with the family—our family—at Gerardo's house tomorrow?"

"I would like that. Thank you."

"We will drive you. My uncle—" He shot Marc a look. "Our uncle lives in Udine."

Drago turned abruptly and left.

"What was that all about?" Libby asked as they headed back to the car.

Marc put his hand on the small of Libby's back to guide her across the cobbled street. "We are not friends, your cousin and I."

"Do ya think? You two were like schoolboys making a fight date to meet after class. To settle the score." Even as she tried to laugh, she knew it sounded false.

In the short time she'd been with Drago and his family, it was apparent that her cousin and Marc were different kinds of men. Where Marc was fun-loving and carefree—most of the time, she amended—Drago was proud and, she suspected, passionate about things. "You don't like him?"

He started to say something, and seemed to change his mind. "I am an Iacome. He is a Loszach."

"What does that really mean, Marc? Why do you say that?"

"It is complicated."

"We're going to be in the car together for the next half hour. Perhaps you could explain it to me?"

He looked down at her with such sad eyes that Libby felt as if she'd pressed him too hard. On the other hand, she really did want to know more about the feud. "Marc?"

"It is not for me to tell you, Libby."

Chapter Eight

"Wouldn't you rather I took my own car?" Libby asked, eyeing her cousin's two-door car. With the three kids, Melena, and Drago, it already promised to be a tight fit. "Or I could go with Vivia?" She so hoped he'd say yes; it promised to be a long drive.

"I have a big car," Drago replied, offended. "The biggest car. Is plenty of room."

By Italian standards, it was big. In a country where many of the streets had been built thousands of years ago at a time when a horse-drawn chariot was the modern mode of travel, it made sense to have narrow cars.

Libby slid into the backseat between Mico, the eleven-year-old, and Lisa, his younger sister. The toddler, Carmela, sat on Melena's lap in the front. With her feet braced on the bump on the floor, Libby had a difficult

116

time keeping her balance as they twisted and turned their way down the mountain.

"Do you like Italia?" Mico asked.

She smiled down at the dark-eyed boy. "Yes. It's beautiful. I went to Venice yesterday."

"It's okay."

"Your English is very good, Mico."

"We study English in school."

Drago spoke up from the front. "He listens to English music too."

That didn't surprise Libby. She'd already noticed that the radios that played in the shops had Italian hosts but aired music with English lyrics.

"When are you going home?" Mico asked.

"Mico." His father used a tone laden with warning. "We ask how long a guest is staying, not when they are leaving. Remember, Loszachs have proper manners."

Libby chose to ignore the exchange. "When I get Nonna's house fixed."

"Do you speak Italian?" the boy asked.

"Not yet, but I'd like to learn."

"My grandmother speaks Slovene and she's teaching it to me."

"I've heard that some of the older people in the village speak that language."

"Not just the older people here," Drago corrected from the front seat. "But all over. This land was not Italia when my parents were babies."

Libby had heard as much. "Slovenia is very close to here."

"Many people—"

"More than one hundred thousand," Mico interrupted.

"—still speak the language of their ancestors. Your ancestors, Elizabetta."

Libby made a sound to show she'd heard her cousin, but at the same time she felt confused. All her life, she'd thought of herself as being from Italian descent. In her most rebellious youth, when she'd been desperate for some sort of claim to fame, she'd even adopted a slightly Italian accent. "It's strange that Nonna never mentioned that."

"She married Geno Zufferlia, from down South," Drago said, as if that explained it all.

"Why does Mattia have to come here?" Mico suddenly demanded.

"Mico," Drago snapped, *"basta!"* The boy frowned and turned his head to look out the window.

Libby wanted to ask him why he said that. What he had against her nonna. Everyone else in the family always spoke so fondly about Mattia. It couldn't be about the Iacome-Loszach history. Maybe she'd be able to get the family to talk about it today, at dinner.

The rest of the drive to Udine passed quietly. Libby watched the scenery. The corn stalks were already waist high, whereas in Canada they barely showed green. They passed a field of landscaping statues, water fountains, gnomes, massive urns, and marble busts of Mussolini.

Drago's uncle Gerardo—her uncle or cousin, she corrected—was a widower in his late sixties. Although his children were grown with homes of their own, he continued to live in the big family house in the old part of Udine. It had an unimposing three-story facade with massive weathered wooden doors.

Drago rapped the fist-shaped knocker, opened the door, and called out to his uncle.

Gerardo turned out to be a large, barrel-shaped man with huge mitts for hands. Libby had been told that he was actually her nonna's nephew, even though they were much the same age, but she'd heard little about him because, she supposed, he didn't live in Croce. Her nonna's nephew. To Libby, relationships were as uncomplicated as grandparents, parents, or siblings. These she understood. Yet here in Italy, family connections were so convoluted, so substantive. Sighing inwardly, Libby decided that for her own peace of mind she would consider anyone over fifty an aunt or an uncle. Under fifty, a cousin. There. As simple as that.

Apparently Uncle Gerardo spoke no English, but once Drago introduced her, Gerardo boomed out a welcome and kissed her soundly on both cheeks.

The next hour passed in a blur of antipasto made with hard chunks of cheese and salami, wine, and loud, unintelligible voices. When dinner was served, the whole crew moved out to the backyard where a long wooden table had been set out under a corrugated metal roof shaded by olive and laurel trees. Gerardo ushered Libby

into the seat to his right. Celia, one of his daughters—
or perhaps a daughter-in-law, Libby never did learn
all of the names or relationships—was able to speak
English.

"Your grandparents never taught you Italian?" Celia
asked. There was no criticism in her tone.

Libby shrugged. "A little, when I was a child. But
they speak, er, spoke English at home. I'm listening to
a tape that teaches Italian whenever I can." She didn't
mention that Enzo had been coaching her as well. And
Marc. In his way.

"And Mattia? Is she well?"

Libby warmed to the subject. "Yes. She is very well.
Looking forward to returning to Croce."

On recognizing Libby's grandmother's name, Gerardo asked Celia to translate. "My father wants to know
how your parents are."

"Very well, thank you." She turned to the head of the
table. She was learning to look at the person she was
addressing rather than at the translator. "I've always assumed my father is named after you, Uncle Gerardo."

Celia answered for him. "My father says he thinks
that is true." Ah! The daughter.

Libby studied Gerardo's face. "There is a strong
family resemblance."

After a stream of Italian, Celia smiled at her father.
"My father says your father must be very handsome. But
he wants to know why Mattia is spending money on the
old house." She moved her hands to hurry her thoughts
along. "What is she thinking?"

"She misses Croce, especially, I think, since Nonno died. She plans to move back, at least for some of the year." Libby still harbored the hope that Nonna would spend time in Canada as well.

Gerardo looked at Drago and a few terse sentences were exchanged.

"What are they saying?" Libby asked. "Is it something about what happened when Nonna was a girl?"

Celia looked uncomfortable. "They're just talking about the house."

"I'm not sure I understand about why the Iacomes and the—"

Suddenly, young Mico spoke up. "We don't think it's right."

"What's not right?" Libby asked.

"That she—this Mattia—is getting the house."

"Mico! *Basta!*"

"It's true," he said sullenly, frowning at his father. "It should be my father's house. He was going to make money from the tourists. Like the Iacomes do."

Gerardo barked out a command that cut off Mico's words. Falling silent, the rest of the table looked chagrined.

Standing, Drago addressed the group. "We do nothing like the Iacomes." His fist contacting the table had the dishes jumping. "We behave like Loszachs. It is the correct way. It is time-honored. These upstarts have nothing but pride to guide them."

Libby's and Drago's eyes met. He held her gaze meaningfully as if to say there would be no argument, and then turned his attention to his son. Libby felt her hackles rise.

"I need to know if Nonna will be welcomed back here. Will everyone, and I mean *everyone*, welcome her?"

A babble of voices rose in assurance. They had great plans for Mattia. What fun they would all have.

As the last fork was returned to its plate, the men pushed their chairs back for comfort's sake, patting their stomachs. Mico imitated the men. The women stood. Each collected a handful of empty dishes and made their way into the house, the little children following at Melena's skirts.

Libby grabbed a clean tea towel and stood at the ready to dry the dishes as they emerged clean and wet from the rinse sink. "Celia, why does everyone in the family have such strong feelings about the Iacomes?"

"Mattia never told you?"

"It never came up. It's only now that she wants to move back . . ."

"I was a long time ago."

"I still want to know what happened."

"You should ask Mattia," Celia said as she turned to take another stack of plates from Melena.

Libby abruptly straightened. "You make it sound as if Nonna did something wrong."

"No! No, it was Leo Iacome. He broke her heart."

"Marc's grandfather? How? Why?"

"It happened so long ago. I don't know the details."

Libby wondered if it was the casual way she had said "Marc's grandfather" that that made Celia wave off her further questions. In the interest of good manners, she didn't bring up the topic again.

The next evening, Libby put down her hairbrush and nodded with approval as she gave herself a once-over in the mirror. Thank heavens for Vivia's tub. Smoothing lotion over her skin, she appreciated the glow the Italian sun was giving it. She had chosen her clothes with care, wanting to look pretty. No point in kicking herself for not packing fewer work clothes and more feminine things. Who knew? The long, white cotton skirt and the turquoise tank did the trick.

Carrying a folded piece of cloth, she stepped through the open double doors of her bedroom and on to the balcony. This view. This spot. She breathed in the air and drank in her surroundings. She would never forget it. Flicking open the red gingham, she smoothed it over the little round table. In its center she placed a hand-painted, ceramic bowl of gorgeous cherries. The two waiting wineglasses shone. Fiddling with a small bouquet of flowers, she set the vase Marc had bought her in Venice in a place of honor. It looked right grouped there on her deep windowsill with a collection of candles. Still humming, she moved from candle to candle bringing each to life with a small flame. The light they cast together with the starlight would encircle them. She had so much to tell him.

Moments later Marc arrived. It was understood. He'd slip up the back way and appear on her balcony just as the sun was setting. Motionless, she allowed his glance to travel the length of her, from her bare toes peeking from under her skirt to the tip of her dark hair. His eyes paused along the way and it thrilled her.

"Carina." His voice purred. Nice.

She stepped toward him and leaned in to greet his waiting mouth. His hand slid down her arm to her wrist and then clasped her hand. Still their lips explored as his hand found the small of her back. A moment later, she eased away. Still hand in hand, she led him to the table.

He had brought wine, as she knew he would. He coaxed the cork from the neck and poured. Shifting in his seat to see her better, he asked the question that spoke of familiarity, of interest, of caring. "How was your day?"

She stretched out her long legs, settling in, and said, "It was another busy one." Her fingers ticked off a list. "The front-loading washer and dryer combo was delivered. The refrigerator and a space heater too. And Enzo has arranged for a cement cistern to arrive later this week." Her hands opened, palms up. "Downstairs still looks like a bomb hit it. I still pick my way around cases of tiles, tins of paint, crates of appliances, and mounds of tools. But, Marc, I love the sense of accomplishment.

"Oh! And the house is all wired for electricity now," she added. "The person from the power company is coming tomorrow to put in the box." On a sigh, she said, "You know, I think I'm going to miss candles."

"Then here, between us, *cara,* we will always pretend. There will be nothing but candlelight for our secret meetings."

Secret meetings. Pretend. She stored the words away for later examination. There was a response to them deep inside but this was not the time.

"I just realized, I'll need to buy light fixtures and lamps. There have never been any in this house. I'll have to go shopping."

Marc topped off their glasses. "There's a huge flea market in the village next Saturday. You could probably get some good buys."

"I love flea markets." It occurred to her that when people in this area sold their old belongings, they meant old. There would likely be some beautiful antiques. "We should make a day of it." When Marc's face dropped, Libby realized she'd made a mistake. What was she thinking? Of course, they couldn't go together. She touched his hand. "Never mind. Our families. Your aunts go to this market, I suppose. And your mother. We can't be seen together."

He held up both palms and shook his head. "I would be proud to be seen with a beautiful woman like you. But yes, it's my mother, and my aunts . . ."

She tilted her head and studied him. So masculine, so cosmopolitan. "You're afraid of your aunts?"

"Yes." His eyes widened comically. "They can be very frightening. But not as frightening as my mother." He rubbed his arms against an imaginary sudden chill.

She smiled, but remained curious. "Where do they think you go on the evenings you spend here?"

He shrugged. "They don't know I go anywhere."

She decided not to pursue it. Nothing was going to ruin

her mood. "Well, for tonight we can enjoy the candle-light. And the starlight." This evening, Libby had felt especially festive, happy and a part of things. She was being to feel Italian. That was it. She fingered the red-and-white gingham cloth.

"What does *basta* mean?" she asked absently.

"Enough. It means enough. It's short for *abbastanza*. Why?"

Libby gave him an abbreviated version of the conversation at the dinner table the previous night. There was no need to mention that his family name had been brought up—in unflattering terms. "At first I thought they were calling him a, uh, bastard. It caught me off guard."

After they shared a chuckle, Marc said, "It sounds like Drago planned to open the house as a rental property like my Aunt Marana."

"No, not like your aunt's." Her reply was automatic. Marc raised one eyebrow as she went on, "I mean to say—it's Nonna's. I don't know why they would think otherwise."

"I expect the inheritance laws are different here than they are in Canada, much more complex."

"You're saying that Drago thought he owned it?"

"He probably does have a part ownership, even if it's just a tiny percentage. It explains why he was always spying on us when we renovated Marana's place."

"Marc." She shook her head and said, her voice tinged with disbelief, "Drago is a busy man. Running the Loszach Bakery is a big job. You should know, with your position at the vineyard. I'm sure you're exaggerating to say he was spying on you."

Libby decided that she'd call her father the next day and discuss these inheritance laws. She'd see what he knew about who owned what.

Marc shrugged, "That's the way it seemed to me. That's all I'm saying."

"In a village this small, everyone must just be very interested in what others are doing. There can't be any harm in that." She remembered the sinking feeling in her stomach last evening when her family asked about her relationship with Marc.

"Did Drago say anything to you about seeing us in Cividale on Saturday?"

"No, not directly. But his wife did." Libby squirmed in her seat, not willing to share the full experience. "Basically, 'Iacome bad. Loszach good.'" She also decided to edit the fact that Melena and the others also warned her to stay away from Marc. But what was the point? Here she was.

"How do you feel about that?" he asked softly.

Suddenly restless, she moved toward him, holding the bowl of cherries. He opened his arms and she slid onto his lap. Tucking her head into his neck for comfort she thought about her answer. She was going to say it was none of their business, but changed her mind. That wasn't quite right. Instead, she said, "It's silly really. Isn't it? Families. What is one to do? I'm not a child."

"No," his voice full of meaning, "you are not a child. And you are right, *cara,* families are complicated."

Their heads, so close, nodded together. They agreed on that. She stayed, held safe in his arms, for a moment longer, and then eased away, to pace.

Where was the festive air now? She wanted it back. She didn't like this heavy turn the evening had taken. There was no time for sadness. No time for regret. She studied him. As Marc's eyes met hers, she saw there none of the humor that gave them light. And then, with deliberation, he straightened in his chair, reached to the bowl, and picked up a cherry by its stem. The candle flame reflected off its glossy surface.

"Look at that color. So red it's almost black. Soon I will grow a Montepulciano grape to make a wine this color."

He swirled his wine under his nose. Libby sat, grateful for the change in subject, reached for her glass and followed his example. She closed her eyes and let the wine's bouquet fill her senses.

"What do you smell?" he asked.

"Caramel." She frowned, hoping that wasn't a bad thing.

He quickly set her mind at rest with a big, wide smile. "So do I."

"You must know wine very well."

He lifted one shoulder. "I grew up drinking it. But I have been criticized for having no nose."

"Is that why you work in the vineyards instead of the plant? And you have a very manly nose by the way." He instinctively rubbed the end of his nose and they laughed.

The playfulness was back.

"I always wanted to work out-of-doors. With the plants themselves. In truth"—he paused and made an elaborate pantomime of looking to see if anyone could hear him—"I always pretend to understand less than I really do. That way, no one pressures me to do wine-tasting tours or work on cement floors all day."

"You are a cagey man." She sipped. "Oh, this is gorgeous."

The bottle of merlot sat at his elbow. He had pronounced the name in the Italian way, stressing the letter *t* at the end. Libby shifted it so she could see the candlelight through its contents. It was a paler, rosier color than the cherry, but still rich.

Everything with Marc seemed rich. Being with him was unlike any other experience she had ever known. This summer romance was an adventure in sensuous living. He always smelled the wine before each sip as if each whiff carried the possibility of heaven. But it wasn't just wine. She'd also seen him relish the flavor of full-bodied coffee and the simple pleasure in a small bowl of sorbet. His eyes held pure delight as they had watched the small bird take flight. The way he looked at her. Yes. There was much sensuous about him.

"You're gorgeous," she said, surprising herself. She sat up straighter. "Is that corny?"

"To say I'm gorgeous? Never!" He laughed and then added, "And you're gorgeous too."

She loved the way his hair fell across his forehead in loose curls. She reached up a finger and played with a section. Marc took her hand and kissed the back of her fingers. An electric pulse surged through her arm and landed in her heart. They locked eyes. She leaned into him, and their lips met. She tasted wine. Sensations of warmth, delight, pleasure, and anticipation filled her. It was the sound of her own moan that brought her back. Reluctantly back.

He stuck the cherry between his teeth, pulled the stem off, and closed his mouth over it. His eyes closed. As she watched him, a proverb popped into her head: It is no use making two bites of a cherry. She promised herself that for the rest of her time there, they would enjoy life to its fullest.

Chapter Nine

Summer solstice, the Feast of St. John the Baptist, midsummer, the longest day of the year . . . The people of the village of Croce, in fact, of this region of Italy, did not consider June 21 to be like any other day. It was a day of celebration, of festivities. Libby could feel it from the moment she woke. Over the last week or so she had heard of little else. And now it was upon them.

The rocky field at the lower edge of the village was alive with activity. There, with the adjacent mountains and sweeping valley lying before it, people contributed dry brush and logs to create a huge mound that soon would become a fire. Its size had grown each time Libby had heard it described—certainly flames would leap several stories high. Heavy wooden planks topped sawhorses to make tables, which in turn were covered with bright tablecloths. In the early evening, people lugged folding chairs, buckets full of ice, and trays of cheeses, waxy prosciutto ham, and other favorites.

"We always provide the breads and sweets," Vivia explained.

Libby adjusted her hold on the other end of the basket, heavy with cellophane-covered loaves and dessert boxes. Libby chimed in with her cousin, "It is a Loszach tradition." They laughed.

As they worked together setting out wooden platters for the breads, men, women, and children stopped to exchange a word. *A word is about right,* Libby thought as she said only *buona sera* and the famous *ciao*, and, of course, her often-repeated *scusa. Non parlo italiano.* She smiled to herself as she wished someone would bring a hammer into the conversation. She could pipe up quite sweetly with *mano* and a few other home renovations goodies. The fact that the villagers didn't seem to mind, and struggled with English for her benefit only made her appreciate them more. In her time there, she had collected a glossary, a list of single words, but no real feeling for sentence structure. And yet, here she was recognized and included. It occurred to her that she had come to feel like part of the village. Apparently she'd been a common enough face these past few weeks that no one felt the need to stare at her or ask where she came from, or to whom she belonged. She had tried to fit in too, using the language where she could and stopping to greet people on the street. Lovely people, she thought as she looked over the growing crowd.

An hour before sunset, the Iacome family arrived. Twenty or so adults and a handful of children trooped onto the field. The moment the children's feet touched the grass, they took off as if sprung from elastics. A soccer ball appeared.

Marc and Enzo set a tin washbasin full of ice on the ground at the end of one table, the length of the field from the Loszachs. Another man shoved bottles of wine among the ice. They'd brought a case of red wine too, as well as glass tumblers, and a half-dozen corkscrews. The traditional Iacome donation.

A cheer went up by the children as the men put a torch to the wood. They would want a steady blaze when the sun had finally set. Libby had read about summer solstice celebrations in Stonehenge. She assumed that the tradition of these fires began from the same pagan beliefs but had, over the generations, evolved to include Christian ideology. By now, the bonfire threw soft waves of heat, and a pleasant, hazy sap perfumed the air. People milled about chatting, drinking wine or beer, and loading paper plates with food.

Libby stood amid the extended Loszach family, but she kept sneaking glances toward Marc. Every now and again, their eyes connected and Marc would wink.

"He's coming over here," Vivia hissed in her ear.

Libby turned, hoping to see Marc approach. Instead, she saw a dignified, elderly man striding purposefully toward her, his eyes pinned on her face. She knew instinctively who he was and studied him in turn. He stood tall and straight with a face that could best be described as aristocratic. And handsome. His full head of white hair was brushed straight back from his high, tanned fore-head. He stopped directly before her.

The man put his fingertips under her chin and turned her head one way, then the other. As odd an encounter as it was, Libby found it was natural to comply. As he stud-ied her, he remained expressionless, and yet, his eyes glistened with tears. Emotion radiated from him. Moved, she took his rough hands in hers.

Vivia stepped forward and made a formal introduction in Italian. Libby's voice was husky as she spoke, "*Buona sera*, Signor Iacome." Yes, this was Marc's grandfather, the patriarch of the Iacome family and the man from Nonna's past.

Leopoldo Iacome bowed and lightly kissed the back of her fingers. When he straightened, he seemed to have overcome his moment of emotion. "I knew your grand-mother. Is she well?" he asked in heavily accented Eng-lish.

"Yes." The single word affirmed both that she was aware of his past connection and that her grandmother was in good health. "She is coming to Croce in a few weeks."

He tilted his head to speak more intimately. "Here. She is coming here."

Libby heard clearly that these were not questions but statements. "Have you spoken—?"

She had been about to ask if Leo had been in touch with her grandmother, but two women had suddenly appeared and flanked Leopoldo. One was Marc's aunt Marana. They didn't acknowledge Libby or Vivia, who had never left her side. He frowned down at them, but listened to their stream of words. Libby didn't understand what they were saying, but it was clear even to her that they wanted him to accompany them. Anywhere else. Leopoldo inclined his head toward both Libby and Vivia, and then he allowed himself to be led away.

A hush had fallen on the group nearest them and all eyes seemed to be on Libby. She scanned the Iacomes for Marc and met his eyes. At that distance his expression was unreadable.

"What was that about?" Vivia whispered in Libby's ear.

"Let's take a stroll and look at the fires." She grabbed her shawl and in the way that was becoming familiar now, Libby hooked her arm through Vivia's and steered her cousin away.

The bonfire roared, shooting three-story-high red and yellow flames toward the sky. The revelers became black silhouettes against its vivid color as Libby and her cousin moved farther away into the darkness.

Now, in the full darkness of night, Libby could see other fires here and there on the mountains and valleys around. They must have been as huge as the Croce flame, because theirs were clearly visible even across what Libby knew were vast distances.

"Spectacular. Are they all having a party tonight?" Libby asked.

"Yes. Even people who have moved to the cities come home for the festival. Libby, what did—"

Out of the darkness Drago appeared. "What do you do here in the dark? And without a drink." He had a bottle of wine in one hand, and two glasses in the other. "You must drink tonight."

"It's not grappa, is it?" She knew better than to accept a tumbler of that. Far too potent for her.

"Vino." He passed her a glass and gurgled the dark liquid into it. He filled the other one he still carried, toasted, and took a deep drink.

"What about me?" Vivia said. "I get no wine?" She shook her head at Libby and made a mock swipe at Drago. They'd grown up together, and knew each other well.

"You have this glass. I will drink from this." He took a swig right from the bottle.

The women exchanged a smile of understanding. Drago had certainly been enjoying much wine. He slung an arm around Libby's shoulder. She tried to be good-natured about accepting his hug, but she couldn't help feeling a little uncomfortable.

"He is not good."

Libby tried to read her cousin's expression but his face remained in shadows. "Excuse me?"

"Marcello Iacome. He is not for you."

"Listen, I know you mean well . . ." She squirmed out of his embrace. "Tell me, what is this thing between the Iacomes and us?"

Drago balled his fist and thumped his chest. "It is in the blood, this difference. We are of the mountain. The Iacomes, they are from Roma, Milano. Not Slovenian, you understand?"

Libby could see that he was perfectly serious—blood, mountains. At any other time, she would have roared with laughter.

"Drago . . . not tonight," Vivia implored.

"No. I don't understand, Drago. I try and I try. But I don't understand. Excuse me." Libby seethed in exasperation and as she walked back toward the merrymakers, she could hear Drago and Vivia in a heated exchange.

Libby headed toward the sound of beckoning voices. She arrived in time to see the crowd move their chairs to encircle two groups of men who sat in rows facing one another. Libby didn't recognize any but Enzo who sat with one side. Suddenly, one man opened his mouth and sang in full volume. A man from the other side replied in a similar tone and melody. Then two men from each side. After a moment, they were all in full throat, but not at the same time. It was if they replied to one another.

Enchanted, Libby moved through the onlookers until she found Mico and Melena and waited for a lull before whispering to Mico, "What are they singing about?"

He shrugged. "Sometimes the fields, sometimes the women."

Libby caught Enzo looking at her. She lifted her palms, giving him private applause. He looked pleased. He had a strong, beautiful voice.

When the singers took a break, other music began and couples moved, hand in hand, toward the center and began to dance. It was lovely. She stood watching for a time and then decided that her time on the sidelines had ended. She would find Marc and ask him to dance. Whether it was the wine, the moon, the solstice itself, or more likely, Drago's stupid chest-thumping speech, Libby felt reckless. Only here would asking a man to dance—an Iacome man, she corrected herself—seem reckless!

Her eyes roamed the crowd. The bonfire flickering had faces first in light, then dark, then light again. It was difficult to see. But she knew generally where he'd be, where all the Iacomes would be. She headed in that direction. As she got closer to the group, she spotted him standing behind an empty chair, just leaning there, watching the dancers. Perhaps he too was scouring the crowd for her. She paused. Instinctively, she ran a hand over the front of her dress, smoothed her hair, and adjusted her pashmina shawl. *I look just fine*, she thought bravely. With her eyes on him, she set off again in his direction. This time it was a hand on her shoulder that had her pausing. She looked to see Vivia's face full of concern. "Libby, don't do this thing."

"Vivia, for heaven's sake. I am just going to dance with him. I like him."

"There will be no dance." Vivia's voice was full of some emotion Libby couldn't understand.

"Please, Viv. I just want to dance."

Libby turned back to find the spot empty where just seconds ago Marc had stood.

"We'll dance. Like at Uncle Gerardo. Let's find Melena."

Croce, 1947

Ever since she was twelve years old, Mattia and her friends had their own parties while the adults enjoyed the annual bonfire lighting on the eve of summer. Now she was old enough to go to the festival as an adult, if she wished. She did not wish. Mattia and Leo had plans of their own.

"You'll get caught," her friend Sophia was saying. "People will wonder where you are."

"The parents will think I'm with the young people. The young people will think I'm at the fire. It's perfect."

"They won't believe that. Not now. People are suspicious of you two."

Mattia paused and studied her friend, her long black hair and dark shining eyes. "I wish you could find someone, Sophia."

"So do I."

Something about her the way her friend avoided looking her in the eye had Mattia wondering. Was her friend so jealous that it was causing a rift in their relationship? She had noticed lately that they no longer spent as much time together. "Have you thought about Gerardo—?"

"Ew," Sophia cried, swatting Mattia playfully. "He's just a boy."

"He's good-looking. At least, so they tell me." To Mattia, Gerardo would always be her baby cousin, even though they were the same age. She also knew that

Sophia carried a soft spot in her heart for Gerardo. "He'll be here tonight, you know. The whole family is coming home for the festival."

Sophia shrugged. "I wouldn't even know what he looked like anymore, he's been gone so long."

"He's bigger now," Sophia said, holding her palms wide to indicate broad shoulders, "and more sophisticated from living in the city."

"I always thought our little school was too backward for him. Not enough sports for him either."

"They tell me he's pretty good at kicking around a ball too. Can't you see him out on the field?"

Sophia's face abruptly changed. "You changed the topic again. Back to Leo."

"If people start to wonder where I've gone, you can take Gerardo and go looking for me. *Up* the mountain. It's clear and the moon will be bright. You won't have any trouble walking. Doesn't that sound romantic?"

Sophia shook her head sadly. "Gerardo would be the angriest, Mattia; you know that to be true. He hates Leopoldo, always has."

"Yes," Mattia conceded. "It's going to be hard to get him to be our friend when Leo and I are married. But he will come around. He's family."

The field at the foot of the village pulsed with activity as people set up the long tables of food and drink. The Iacomes always brought the wine. The Loszachs supplied baked goods. The women of both communities cooked every other kind of food. As Mattia watched the children running circles around one another, she considered how much she'd grown up in the past year. She was a woman, a woman in love. She smiled at them indulgently.

For the next hour, Mattia enjoyed the familiar sight of the lighting of the bonfire. As she and her friends had done every year, she stood at the edge of the steep incline and discussed the blazes that dotted fields around the other villages in the distance. They ate and drank and laughed and listened to the men warming up the accordions. All the while, Mattia covertly searched for Leo. When she judged that she had stayed long enough, she searched out her mother.

"Have you had enough to eat?" her mother asked.

She nodded. "I'll make a basket up to take back with the children."

Her mother studied her. "You don't need to leave, you know. There will be other boys and girls your age here tonight."

"I know. I'm not in the mood." Although Mattia kept her eyes averted from her mother, she felt suspicion radiating off the woman. She rubbed her lower abdomen in a motion that all women understood. "I'm not feeling well."

Very rarely had Mattia ever deceived her mother, and the sensation of guilt gnawed at her so that by the time she herded the younger children of her extended family up to the house, her stomach really did feel ill. There, she kissed her grandmother on the cheek and then, after grabbing a handful of matches and a candle, made her escape.

Festival night transformed Croce. Sweet-smelling smoke wafted up from the fields. Men's voices echoed off walls. The streets and alleys, normally deserted at this time of night, were bright with lights and sounds.

Mattia had intended to scurry down to the path between the woods and the village as quickly as possible, but as she neared a small square off to the edge of town, she heard strange male voices. She peeked around the corner. Two young men stood with their backs to her, their bodies silhouetted by the white stone of the church. They seemed to be talking quietly to someone who sat on the church steps, but she couldn't make out who it was because of the dark shadows.

Mattia grew up during the war. Active fighting had long ceased, but the politics of the situation still festered. Even tonight, during the hubbub of the festival, the sight of two strange men had her heart in her throat. As she spied on them, she wondered what it was about them that that her heart thudding in her ears. Two young men, good-looking judging by the way their clothes hung on their frames.

Then she heard Sophia's giggle. Her suspicion turned to concern. She silently walked toward the tableau.

Sophia gasped. "Mattia?"

"What are you doing sitting here in the dark?" She wanted to get a better look at these men so she dug her candle and matches from the deep pockets of her skirt.

One of the men asked, "Who's your friend?" His Italian was correct, but there was something odd about his accent.

Sophia had scrambled to her feet and down to the

street level. She breathlessly introduced Mattia to her friends, Dan and Tony. By now, Mattia had her candle lit. The men were in their mid- to late twenties, wore loose trousers with leather belts, open-collared shirts, and had very short hair. Military-cut hair. Mattia instantly knew who they were: American soldiers from what was now called the Free Territory of Trieste.

United States soldiers. The enemy.

Appalled, she grabbed at her friend's elbow. "Come away, Sophia."

Sophia jerked out of reach. "These are friends of mine."

"They're Americans. What if someone sees you?" She quickly snuffed out the candlelight.

"Tony is just as Italian as you and me."

"Please, Sophia—"

"You of all people should understand!"

"I understand it's dangerous."

"Go meet your precious Leo and leave me alone."

Croce, present day

The party was in full, raucous swing. Libby had danced with her cousins; even Drago joined them in a loose freestyle kind of dancing. They had laughed as they danced, and other than the moment with Drago, it had been a fun evening. She enjoyed herself, but the language differences proved very tiring. Libby slipped away.

She tucked her shawl around her and meandered toward home. The streets were dark and quiet, but by now she knew her way around the serpentine paths and narrow alleys. When she put her hand against a wall for balance as she climbed some stairs, she was surprised to find that the stone still held some of the day's heat. It felt comforting.

She hadn't expected to feel this way about the village. Maybe Drago's point about the Loszach clan being of the mountain had some truth. This place really did get into your blood. She shook aside the notion. In this day and age, no one's bloodlines were purely one type, of one vein. There had been intermarriages for thousands of years. Still, some things felt instinctual.

She rounded the corner to her own street, singing the only Italian song she knew, even vaguely. There was the moon and a pizza pie. Although only a sliver of a moon glinted in the sky, it reflected off the white cement and pale gray cobbles. A dark shape waited on Libby's stoop.

She sighed out his name, "Marc."

He unfolded slowly. "You stayed there longer than I expected."

"It's a good party."

He reached around to unlatch the gate to the external stairway as if he took the invitation to her balcony for granted. Libby pulled her lower lip between her teeth. Was it smart to be near him now, with the wine humming in her system?

He must have seen her hesitation. "We need to talk, Libby."

"Talk?" It wasn't talk she was interested in.

"About my family."

She exhaled and followed him up the stairs. "Your family. I met your grandfather. But then you know that. He is striking." He might want to talk about family but she didn't. She'd had enough. "Marc, why did you leave the celebration this evening?"

He didn't answer right away, but pulled out a chair and held it for her. Then he sat across from her.

"I walk when I need to think," he explained. One half of his handsome face stayed hidden in shadows, but both eyes glistened. "I've been thinking about us. The way we sneak around."

That was exactly the right word, Libby thought. Sneaking. But she merely nodded.

"It's like Romeo and Juliet, yes?"

"You'll remember, Marc, that didn't end well."

Here they were together, once again, on the balcony, their place of refuge. She wrapped her shawl tighter to her, tucking her arms beneath the shawl's gentle fabric.

Out over the darkness, a bonfire glowed in the distance. Some far-off village was sharing the delight of the festival. In that grouping, Libby knew, some young lovers danced, holding each other close, whispering secret longings. They would hold each other shamelessly, in front of knowing, approving, encouraging family. They were part of the whole. Not like Marc and her. Fragments.

She sighed. She knew Marc was lighting the candles, decanting the wine. The music from the Croce bonfire drifted in the evening air. On the breeze she could still hear the men's voices, bass and full. Somehow sweet, somehow heartbreaking.

Marc was beside her, offering her wine. The wine he created, his family created, from vine to grape to this glorious drink. She sipped, held it in her mouth, and closed her eyes. Its richness teased her tongue, begging her to take it in. She resisted, waiting. She wanted to remember it. Forever. So that in time she would be able to close her eyes and allow her heart to carry her here, to this moment. No matter where she was or what paths her life had laid before her, she could transport herself to this very spot.

"Mio amore." My love. Marc came behind her and wrapped his arms around her. He held her. Again, she closed her eyes. "You are sad."

"No, not sad," Libby said in truth. "Perhaps melancholy, perhaps yearning, perhaps . . ."

He bowed his head, laying a cheek to hers. She could feel its texture, the slight roughness of it. Moving her cheek against his, she reveled in the simple masculinity of it. She sank closer into his chest, feeling his warmth envelope her.

"I wanted to dance with you this evening. In the firelight. No matter who was there. Just us, dancing." Her voice caught with the longing.

Marc turned her, never letting her go, keeping her close. He folded his arms around her and began to sway, slowly. Libby tucked her head in under his chin, laid her cheek against his chest and, with a smile, found the rhythm. She began to move with him. As his hand slipped under her hair and across her neck, she raised her face to him. Parting her lips, knowing what awaited, his mouth covered hers. The sweetness, the hesitancy of the joining kindled a flame within her core. Slowly, his hands moved from her neck, tracing her outline from shoulders to waist to hips. Still they danced.

In the distance, the singers began another song. Their clear voices were carried by the wind to serenade these two dancers.

Chapter Ten

The next morning Libby gave quiet thanks for the thing that had changed most since she arrived in Italy. Indoor plumbing! She hummed as she made her ablutions, slipped into her work uniform of low-slung jeans and a T-shirt, and wound her hair up in something resembling a knot.

Enzo arrived early. Today was the day they were going to tackle the construction of the interior stairwell.

"You have a beautiful voice, Enzo." Holding her hand over her heart to emphasize the point, she tried again. "For *cantare,* singing. You and the other men sounded lovely." She was used to saying the same thing several ways now. He would understand one version if not the other. He got the message on the last try and his cheeks became rosy.

"You had fun last night, Leeeby?" It was darling how he pronounced her name.

"Oh, yes. I had fun."

This time Enzo looked directly at her. She felt the depth of his gaze. It was a brief but meaningful glance that he broke to lean over his toolbox. His head gave an almost imperceptible shake.

Well, chat time is over apparently. Yup, I'm all talked out, she thought as she made herself busy. Slipping on her leather work gloves, she assured herself that the scenes playing in her head were just that—in her head. He couldn't possibly know.

They got to it. First, they marked out where the bottom step should be located so it didn't impede on the space and traffic flow of the parlor below, then they worked out the angle to allow for a landing, and drew the opening on the second floor. After an ear-splitting chainsaw did its work, a gaping hole on a second-floor bedroom looked down into the first floor.

Libby picked at the rough edge of the thick planks with her finger. It would need some type of edge banding.

"Walnut," Enzo said. He reached for a jigsaw to tidy up the hole.

Impressed that he knew the English word for the wood, she replied in Italian, *"E grande, spesso."*

"The trees grow here." He made a sweeping motion with his hands.

She tried to say that in Italian, *"Il alberi crescono qui."* The way he patted her shoulder left her wondering what exactly she had just said.

Just then, a high voice sounded from downstairs. *"Permesso?"*

Libby glanced at her watch and realized they had been at it for several hours. She left by the exterior door, skipped down the stairs, and met Drago's son at the bottom. "Come in, Mico."

"My mother sent you this."

He carried a plate covered with a linen tea towel. Libby lifted the corner. "Hmmm. Cookies. Please tell her thank you. Would you like one?"

"Yes, please."

"How about a glass of milk?"

"Yes. I am to say that your grandmother called my mother. She wants you to call her."

Libby tensed. "Is anything the matter?"

He shook his head as much to say he didn't know as to reply to the question. "She called you here; you did not answer."

Her eyes took in the cellular phone's recharger. She silently cursed her lack of discipline with it. "I don't have the cell phone turned on. Here, let me get you some milk, and then I'll call Nonna."

Like all boys his age, Mico looked like he wanted to finish every cookie on the plate. He'd swallowed the first before Libby finished pouring the milk.

While Mico, glass in one hand and cookie in the other, looked around the house, Libby tapped out the long trail of numbers necessary to call to Canada. "Hello, Nonna. Is everything okay?"

"Yes, I just wanted to call you for a change."

Libby settled in a chair. "Did you get the color chips? Do you like them?"

"Yes, but you don't need to go to the trouble of mailing them here. You have wonderful taste—we like the same things." She chuckled at her compliment to herself. "Your father printed out the pictures too. The tiles look beautiful."

"Don't they? I loved the colors together. We're working on the inside staircase right now. They're just going to be very plain and simple. I'll shoot some digital pictures of it too and zip them along next time I'm in Cividale."

"There's no rush. Is there much more to do?"

Libby looked around the cozy kitchen and mentally shrugged. "It's actually very comfortable now. Mind you, I haven't started on the second floor or the master bedroom. The downstairs still needs a few small things, like a towel rod and lamps. Would you like me to wait until you get here so we can buy them together?"

"It doesn't matter either way. We can shop together but if you see something you like in the meantime, I know it will be perfect."

Libby kissed her fingertips loudly into the phone. "*Perfetto!* As they say here Nonna. Marc says there's a flea market here this coming weekend and that I'll probably be able to get some bargains."

Nonna's sigh carried across the miles. "The flea markets. I remember them. What fun they are."

As her grandmother chatted on, Libby realized that she could hear Enzo and Mico talking. At first she thought nothing of it. Then she tensed. Mico probably knew who Enzo was, which family he came from. What kind of fire would she have to put out if it became known that an Iacome was in a Loszach's house? Good Lord.

"Nonna," she said, "could you hold a moment?"

Mico had gone into what would eventually be the sitting room but at the moment more resembled a demolition site: stacks of wood, metal boxes opened with tools spilling out, a broom leaned against the wall next to a mound of wood chips and sawdust. The two appeared to be getting along. In fact, Enzo seemed to be demonstrating how he would bolt the new staircase to the support posts.

Libby carried the phone outdoors onto the poor, neglected terrace. As her eyes scanned the almost hidden brick pattern, she promised herself to get at it, one of these days . . .

"I told you that Enzo, Marc Iacome's . . . well, I guess he's some kind of distant cousin and his closest friend, is working here?" She looked about as she talked, but the only person she could see was a woman hanging laundry on a rod affixed to a second-floor window. "Do you think that people will make a fuss about that when they find out?"

"Here, in Canada, I would have laughed at that thought. But in Croce? Well, probably."

"I'm sorry, Nonna. I hope I haven't caused you a problem."

"Me? Don't worry about me."

"When you get here, people will already be talking about you."

Nonna laughed. "I think I'll be giving them lots of other things to talk about."

The temperature had climbed higher than usual for this time of the day, so Libby chose a section of wall in shade to lean against. The startling white walls reflecting in the sunlight made the shadow seem that much blacker. "I met a man who knows you at the bonfire last night." She hesitated, not sure how to go on.

"Oh?" The tension in that one word spoke volumes.

"Leopoldo Iacome."

"How is he?"

"He looks well. Handsome. Dignified." Libby's voice took on a teasing ring. "He's a silver fox, Nonna."

"Is his hair gray?"

"White, actually. Nonna, what's the deal with you two? The look on his face . . . It was like he was seeing you and not me."

"Sweetheart. Years ago," her voice faltered, "I was going to marry him. Things got very crazy then and I left him. I left Italy. I didn't even say good-bye. To my everlasting regret."

Libby felt stung for her grandfather's sake. "What about Nonno?"

"Oh, I don't mean I didn't love your grandfather. I loved him very much. But, well, with Leo it was, ah, different."

"What happened?"

"I was young and hurting."

"You were hurting? Why? What did he do to you?" Libby could see Nonna, so young and beautiful—the woman in the wedding photograph. Then she imagined her hurt, tears, and heartache. The sudden pain the image caused awakened something within her. Deep inside Libby a momma lion started to pace, ready to pounce, to protect.

"Nothing. Leo did nothing. Nothing that a million other boys his age didn't do then." Her heavy sigh carried through the phone. "Libby, *cara,* dear, it was a different time. And in a different place, a different culture. Let's not talk about this."

"But if you're moving here, maybe it would be best to clear the air now. I could lay some groundwork for you."

"My sweet child." Nonna chuckled. "That is so much like you. You don't have to take on any of this. As I said, it was a lifetime ago. Almost." With a new resolve, she continued, "Thank you, but no. Now, about your suggestion for the floor. I like it. But don't worry if it is not finished. I will have lots of time."

She chatted on for a few more minutes without pause, talking of news from home, as if to discourage Libby from asking more about Leopoldo Iacome. Libby knew Nonna. The subject was closed.

Libby sent her love and disconnected. Standing in the shade, she stared at the phone in her hand. Perhaps if she had explained that she had a very personal reason for wanting to ease the tensions between the Loszachs and the Iacomes, Nonna would have told her the full story.

Her hand ran over the stonework of the wall. Her heart whispered for Marc. Instead of Nonna and Leo, her mind pictured Marc and herself. Heartbroken. It was too much. She shook her head and cleared away the image. Well, there were other ways to find out the Loszach side of the story.

She moved back indoors, calling to Mico. "Let's go to your house."

Mico sat at the kitchen table staring sheepishly at the last cookie. "Why?"

"I'm going to return this empty plate." She bit into the one remaining cookie. She raised one brow pointedly at Mico and headed toward the sitting room. The jigsaw ground into a length of wood, making verbal communication impossible. Pointing at her watch and using her fingers to flash up thirty minutes, she explained to Enzo that she would be gone for a little while. She turned back to the kitchen.

"Mico, I want you to come with me, to translate. That's the least you can do for eating all my cookies." She tweaked his ear playfully and headed out the door.

As they wound their way around the narrow alleys and cobbled streets toward Drago and Melena's house, Mico seemed quieter than usual. Libby wondered if he had recognized Enzo, and knew he was from the Iacome clan.

"What do you think of the house?" Libby asked him.

The boy shrugged. "It's messy. It's okay."

"I saw you talking to the workman." She looked down at his face, but Mico just shrugged again. "Do you know him?"

Lynn M. Turner

"I know who he is." He shot her an insultingly disgruntled look, as if he were the adult and she the child. "Why do you let him into our house?"

Libby noted that he'd said "our house," a Loszach house presumably. "Why shouldn't I? He does good work. He charges a fair price."

"No, he doesn't."

"And you know that—how?"

"He's not our kind of people."

"What kind of people is he?"

He looked as if he had a bad taste in his mouth. "Iacome."

"Oh, Mico." He'd already been indoctrinated into the feud. She wanted to take him by the shoulders and shake him. Instead she offered, gently, "Do you know what prejudice means? It means deciding that you don't like someone before you've even met them. You prejudge them. How sad to think there could be people who feel that way about you. They might never know how nice and clever you are—and how many cookies you can eat." She tousled his hair and hoped a shred of reason touched him.

Now that Drago and Melena's house was in sight, Mico took to his heels and ran home. Of course he'd tell his parents about Enzo, Libby thought. And why shouldn't he? Would Drago object? She gritted her teeth. If Drago had the gall to say anything, she'd be ready for him. He had no right to tell her whom she should hire. And this prejudice because someone happened to come from a certain family was ridiculous. Talk about the sins of the fathers!

She took a moment to calm herself. Who was she kidding? She wouldn't fight with him. She'd just say something like, "He's a good worker." That'd do. She'd only be there a few more weeks. An unexpected stab of sadness wounded her solar plexus.

Libby squared her shoulders and rapped on the open door, "*Ciao*, Melena?"

"*Entrare*, Libby," Melena's voice called.

The house had been built around a central hall with the kitchen taking the entire width in the rear. Judging by the low ceilings and stone exterior walls, it appeared to be approximately as old as the others in the village, but had undergone many renovations. The hallway, for example, had been split into two to accommodate a stairwell with a much gentler slope than the one Enzo was installing in Mattia's house.

In the kitchen, Libby set the plate on the table and said, "*Grazie.*"

Carmela, Melena and Drago's youngest child, played happily on a blanket in the corner. Libby crouched down beside her and rubbed the toddler's soft hair.

"*Caffè*, Libby?" Melena asked with a smile.

"*Sì, grazie.*"

Libby peeked into the living room, but Mico had made himself scarce.

Melena set about getting the coffee made. "Mattia? *Telefonata?*"

"*Sì, sì, grazie.*"

Libby took a couple of steps back down the hall and called up the stairs, "Mico, would you come here and translate for us, please?"

The boy clomped noisily down the stairs and into the kitchen where he obediently sat on a chair at the table. He looked at the cookies and back at his mother. She gave him permission with a nod. Once she had the coffee over the heat, she fetched a plate from an open hutch and proceeded to load it with cookies, which she then placed in front of Libby.

"Mico, please tell your mother that I'd like her to tell me what she knows about my grandmother and what happened between her and Leo Iacome."

Mico sat straighter and translated. Then he continued talking for a bit longer. Amid the rapid flow of Italian words, Libby heard Enzo Iacome's name. At that, Melena darted an eye toward Libby, then focused on her son again. She sat down, put her hands on the top of the table, and folded them together. When Mico stopped, Melena took on an inward look, exhaled so her breath lifted her bangs, and started talking.

Chapter Eleven

Marc Iacome was in a state. It had been an awful day. He stopped pacing the length of his house, stared out the window at the mountains, and thought of last night. Of Libby. Of how it felt to hold her in his arms. Right. It had felt right. And since he thought of little else that entire day, he had paraded around the vineyards, the winery, and in and out of the boardroom like Napoleon on a campaign. One hand tucked in—protecting himself where he was most vulnerable. His heart.

He had to see her. This was crazy. He had tried to call but that stupid little phone wouldn't connect. He'd speak to her about that. Make no mistake! What was the point in buying the thing if she wasn't going to use it? He raked his hand through his hair.

Hours had passed now since he'd kissed her sweet lips and swayed to the haunting music.

He moved toward his closet to grab his rain jacket. If it hadn't started to rain yet, it would soon. The smell of the air's heat had promised it. Shrugging into the slicker, his glance fell on the tickets in the copper tray by the entranceway. Two tickets to the opera in Verona. He had ordered them as a gift to his mother. But this afternoon it had hit him like a thunderbolt. Instead of giving them to his mother, he would make them a gift to Libby tonight. For his mother's birthday, he'd had another brainwave. It was all taken care of now. All he had to do was make sure Libby wanted to take the trip with him. They could have time together, away from the village, and really enjoy each other's company.

Willing this nuisance of a headache aside, he stepped out into the rain and shifted his hood over his head. The walk would do him good. He needed a chance to clear his head, to shake away the shreds of his work that plagued him. Most, he needed to set to rest this constant nagging that went on inside his head. It was about Libby. It was about his family. The Iacome name. The Loszach name. Their differences were so great.

Even as he trudged along the path that he and Enzo had blazed, he comforted himself with the notion that Libby wasn't really a Loszach. She was certainly one step removed at least. Even her grandmother, the famous Mattia Loszach, had been away from her people for so long now that she would have learned new ways.

Marc had only been a boy the first time he heard Mattia's name spoken. It was in hushed tones, a secret shared between his mother and Deborah, his grandmother. He had stood at the kitchen door understanding nothing but the anger simmering in the tone they used. The child's curiosity had been piqued. He had waited until bath time when he and his mother were alone to ask what Mattia Loszach meant. His mother shushed him ferociously and made him promise never to utter the name in the house again. As he slid into the tub that night he felt very satisfied at least to know that Mattia Loszach was a name, not a thing.

He guessed that it was that same boy within him, the one left to guard a secret he didn't understand, that made him so loath to mention Mattia's granddaughter to his mother. And what was there to tell really?

That evening, a sudden storm enveloped the village. Libby reached up, unlatched a window casement, and pulled it open. Outside, the rain dropped in vertical sheets but even if it hadn't, the stairs to the second story sheltered this spot. It amazed her that here, high in the mountain, the wind rarely blew and the trees grew tall and straight. The cool, moist air smelled delicious after the heat of the day. She leaned her elbows on the kitchen's deep window ledge, her chin resting on her hands. She knew she wouldn't see him this evening. A long walk, uphill, in the rain. Unless he used her front door, the hillside would be slick with mud. She was determined not to feel disappointment.

Instead, leaning on the windowsill, she breathed deeply and let her mind go where it wanted. She allowed herself the daydream of walking with Marc hand in hand through the flea market in the sun. And yes. People would stare. But in surprise, not disapproval. They would find a perfect thing to buy and in happiness, kiss each other. Just like any other couple. He'd sling his arm around her as they strolled. People would stop and chat to them. She stood and stretched. It could happen, she told herself. She was already making friends here in Croce. She was beginning to feel very much at home. She was confident that if she had a chance to chat with Marc's mother or one of his scary aunts, she could charm them. She could picture them laughing together, and accepting her. Marc would be so pleased. Her eyes roamed the kitchen. Perhaps she'd make herself some hot chocolate and clear a spot in the sitting room to finish her daydream. Everything was *perfetto* in daydreams.

Reaching to pull the window closed she heard the squelch of footsteps in the mud. She straightened, more curious than frightened. Then Marc appeared. He wore a rain jacket with the hood up so he didn't immediately see her. He was smiling to himself. He was such a happy man; it made her glow just to be around him.

"Marc," she called. Seeing her, his eyes widened with pleasure. He stepped into the shelter under the stairs. "I didn't think you'd come in this weather."

He scoffed. "The rain, it will not keep me from you."

He leaned in and kissed her on the lips. Then he grinned. "See, we are Romeo and Juliet."

"You didn't climb up to my balcony."

He shrugged. "And it's a good thing. You aren't on your balcony."

Laughing, she shoved at him though the window. Delight raced through her. "Come on in. Are you chilled? I'll get you a hot drink."

"Not coffee. I had coffee all afternoon."

She watched as he shook the raincoat out the door before hanging it on a hook. Then he heeled off his muddy sneakers. Moisture had darkened his jeans and molded them to his muscled legs. She stepped up to him and without fanfare, threw her arms around his neck and planted a kiss on his beautiful lips.

"I am so happy to see you." She spoke as much to herself as him. She kissed him again. His eyes shone with pleasure when he looked at her. Still half in the world of her own creation, she imagined him coming home to her, after work. Without missing a beat, she asked, "Why did you have coffee all afternoon? Don't you work outside when it's raining?"

"Bah, meetings, meetings, meetings. I'm going to buy better lighting for the boardroom. The fluorescent lights, they flicker and give me a headache."

A crease formed between her eyebrows. "Would you like a painkiller?"

He shook his head. "It's going away. The walk did me good."

"Sit, sit." She eased out a chair. He followed orders.

She stood behind him and massaged his temples. Marc groaned and leaned his head back. She felt the weight and warmth against her belly. Her heartbeat skipped. Marc reached for one of her hands, pulled it around, and kissed the inside of her wrist. She felt sure he could feel her pulse fluttering under his lips.

His voice was soft as he spoke, taking on a faraway quality. "We always talk about Romeo and Juliet. Have you ever been to Verona, Libby?"

"And gone to see Juliet's balcony, you mean? You do know," she teased, "that Romeo and Juliet were fictional characters."

"Ah, but Shakespeare drew them from the streets of Verona. He, ah"—Marc paused, lifted his hands, and pressed his fingertips together—"he breathed in Verona and breathed out Romeo and Juliet."

"It inspired him."

Even as her hands continued their massage, Marc nodded. "I want to take you there. There is an opera next week. You will go with me?"

She moved to stand in front of him. "Mmmm, an opera in Verona. I've heard about them. Do you have tickets already?"

His eyes twinkled with pleasure as he nodded. "Tickets for two."

"I would love to go with you. Thank you. When is it? Is it formal?" She'd have to go to the nearby city of Trieste to buy a dress. Aw shucks! Shopping? A new dress? Oh, the hardships one has to endure.

"Some people wear formal, but most do not. It is up to you."

"Do you own a tuxedo?"

He lifted one shoulder in a shrug and his eyes sparkled. "I have been told I look very handsome in a tux."

Libby didn't doubt it. The man looked handsome in everything he wore. "Then we will be formal."

Her heart pounded with excitement. She knew very little about opera, but she'd heard that people flocked to Verona because of the setting: a two-thousand-year-old Roman arena. Opera under the stars.

She clapped her hands together in delight. "It's a date! Now. Can I get you some cocoa to drink? I was just going to make some."

"Hot chocolate? I would love hot chocolate."

She busied herself with the milk, the mugs, and the chocolate. While it all heated, she stood facing the stove, her back to the room, to him, and shoved the tips of her trembling fingers into her pockets. His eyes were on her. She could feel them.

"So," she said aloud, drawing out the word. Be normal. Be light. "Did you see Enzo today?"

"No. But he tells me you two understand each other better these days?"

"He's teaching me Italian and I'm helping him with his English. You'd be surprised how much it helps to pass the time when you're sawing or painting."

"Show me what you have been working on these days together."

Cocoa in one hand, Marc draped his other arm over Libby's shoulder and ushered her into the sitting room. "Ah, the stairs are done."

"It's still rough looking," Libby said, gazing up. She could see the window in the upstairs doorway from this angle, and the rain running down the glass. Even on a dreary evening, it allowed light to enter, a benefit she hadn't even considered in the planning stage.

Marc thumped the side of his fist on the six-inch supporting beam. "Very solid."

"Enzo says it's local wood."

Marc nodded. "He found it in his father's place. Good and dry. It won't warp."

She grimaced. Enzo had taken it from his father? She sincerely hoped he had the man's permission.

Libby flicked a switch and the stairwell flooded with light. Eager to show him all she'd accomplished, Libby dashed upstairs and headed across to an inner door. "Nonna will sleep through there."

They moved into the biggest room in the house, with high ceilings opening to the attic—Libby's bedroom only took up half the third story—and multipaned windows that overlooked the village. It was simply decorated with a large, pine wardrobe, twin beds, and two bedside tables. An oriental carpet Libby had found and cleaned was spread welcomingly over the polished wood floor. She moved to the center of the room. "I just finished painting it this afternoon. I'm going to get some curtains, maybe lacy ones since this room doesn't face the morning sun. And I'm going to search for some lamps at the flea market. And art, of course. I know she'll love it." She spread her arms and twirled around. "Can a room be spacious and cozy? This is . . ." She stopped midstream, laughing. "I get so caught up," she said, half apologizing.

Marc moved to take her hand. He was impressed. She could see it on his face. "You've done a wonderful thing here, Libby. Getting this house ready for your grandmother, I mean. Not just the time you spent on it, but the attention to detail. You've got a great eye."

"It's easy when you're working with someone else's money." She laughed to disguise the pure, sweet pleasure his praise gave her. "Those brochures and things you brought me in the beginning were a huge help. It saved me so much time and . . ."

He reached for her hand. "Come to my house for dinner tomorrow night." He asked her so spontaneously that it surprised him as much as it did her. "I want you to see my house, tell me what you think."

"Are you sure? I'd love to. What time and what should I bring?"

"Come when you and Enzo finish for the day. Bring nothing. I will cook for you." Touching the walls again, admiring the soft, warm yellow she chose, he said softly, "Mattia Loszach. She will be very pleased."

Libby raised an eyebrow. "Mattia Zufferlia, Marc. She's been Mattia Zufferlia for fifty-three years." And that, she thought with resignation, was the segue she needed to bring up a subject she'd rather not.

"Come on Marc. Let's go downstairs. I'll make us some more hot chocolate and a bite to eat. We need to talk."

In her kitchen once again, Libby set a cutting board and bread knife on the table. *Bang! Rumble, rumble.* Thunder. She jumped, and then laughed. She automatically counted until the flash of lightning. "Seven seconds. The storm is close."

"Are you afraid of it?" he asked.

"Thunder and lightning? No, I'm not afraid. It made me jump though." She chuckled at herself. After another rumble and boom, she said, "It's louder here on the mountain."

"My grandmother, Deborah—even as a boy I called her Deborah, not Nonna—she used to be terrified. I used to go up to her rooms to sit with her in storms."

Cheese, salami, and pears joined the heavy bread she'd already set out. "What about your grandfather? Leopoldo? Why didn't he sit with her?"

"She said I made her feel better, is all." He lifted one shoulder. "It was tradition."

"Do you miss your grandmother?" She sat across from him trying, without success, to imagine life without her own nonna.

He thought for a moment. "Deborah was a bitter woman. Harsh, always angry. Not to me, but I think inside she was angry." He reached for a piece of cheese. "My mother misses her though, and I don't like to see her unhappy."

Libby noticed that he rubbed his stomach and slid the plate closer to him.

"Your mother misses her?" A woman missing her mother-in-law. That said something nice about Anna Iacome.

"You see, my grandfathers worked together—my mother's father worked for Leo, so my mother grew up always around the Iacomes. Her own mother died when she was very young. My mother learned much from

Deborah. Then my mother married my father—the son of the house—so these two women knew each other for years. My mother was loyal to Deborah, understood her." He stilled and gave her a serious look. "That is why she doesn't . . . ah . . . like you—your grandmother. You see, Deborah always blamed Mattia for her unhappy marriage."

"Did he still love her, even after he married Deborah?"

He lifted his shoulders in one of his expressive shrugs. "Love, the past, it is not something I would have ever talked with him about, you understand?"

Libby did understand.

"But let's not talk about these things." He lifted his eyebrows and grinned. "My mother's birthday is coming soon. I am going to buy her a tree."

"A tree?"

"I think she will be pleased. It is a very different gift than I usually get her. I don't know what you call it in English. The leaves have three colors on them: white, green, and pink."

"I think it's a tricolored beech tree. They're lovely."

He extended his hand over his head. "This one is huge, almost fully grown. They had it planted in a big pot, but it's outgrown that, so they put it up for sale. It will be delivered on her birthday."

He sipped his fresh cocoa and munched for a moment on a piece of the pear.

As the thunder sounded, closer this time, she was grateful they were there this evening, together in the solid house. Her nonna's house.

Libby cleared her throat.

"I spoke to Nonna about your grandfather today."

Marc, who had been reaching for the bread, stopped. "What did she say?"

"Not very much I'm afraid, except that she regretted leaving the way she did, without saying good-bye or anything, and that at the time she was hurting."

"Hurting?" He sawed into the bread with a vengeance.

"He hurt her. Did you know that?"

His beautiful, chocolate brown eyes met Libby's. "And this is her side of the story. He hurt her and she left Italia."

Libby started as the room brightened with lightning. Marc reached a hand toward her, but she pretended she didn't see it. Physical contact with this man would only distract her.

She continued as though he hadn't spoken. "So I went to see Melena. She told me that Leo had denounced a friend of Nonna's. Something about her girlfriend going about with an American soldier after the war."

He sat back, knife in hand, and stared hard at Libby. "Was she?"

"I don't know. Does it matter? Was that such a terrible thing to do?"

"The Americans were our enemy then."

"Not then. That would have been years after peace had been declared."

"Libby, you can't just say, 'There, it is now peace' and expect things to go back to normal. For politicians perhaps. For ordinary people, it is not so easy."

"But for a young girl to go out with a soldier . . . It seems so innocent."

"To us now, yes. But not then. With the war just over, all the death, the hatred."

She conceded the truth in that, but it didn't change her argument. "Our grandparents were hardly more than children." Libby did a quick calculation. "Nonna would have been seventeen."

"Things were different then. Girls married younger. And girls who took up with foreign soldiers were outcasts. Maybe there was more to it than that? Maybe your grandmother was cheating on Leo with a soldier."

Her chin jerked up. "No. When you meet her, you will see that my grandmother would never have been like that. Besides, Melena said that it was Nonna's best friend who was accused, not Nonna. And that it was Leo who denounced her. The girl was forced from the village, never to see her family again."

"But if it were true, Libby—"

"What difference could it have made? The war was over. It seems to me that he tarnished a poor girl's reputation, and what good did it do? He didn't accuse her of spying, which I can see he'd feel duty-bound to speak out about."

Mystified, Marc asked, "And this is the reason she left my grandfather at the altar? Because he . . . er . . . gossiped about her friend?"

"I can't understand it myself. But this is what Melena said. Leo and Mattia were engaged to be married. And yet he caused his fiancée's best friend to be shamed."

She shook her head in disbelief. "He must have known how it would affect Nonna, and he did it anyway."

"Libby, *cara*, they were under pressure, yes?"

She blew out a breath she wasn't aware she was holding. "Because of their families not getting along." She thought again about what Drago had said. The Loszachs were of the mountains and the Iacomes of the cities, of Italy. The bad feelings must have begun long before her grandmother's day. Perhaps it dated all the way back to the days before Italy was unified, to when it was simply a cluster of city-states.

"Maybe the business with the girl and the soldiers was just, as they say, the straw that broke the camel's back."

Libby nodded, thinking. "You're right. Nonna's father was probably ready to grab his family and move the instant that he could get Nonna to agree. Before she could really think about it."

The storm was right overhead. The thunder crashed and lightning flared.

"Perhaps," she continued, "no Loszach would want his daughter to marry an Iacome. Not then."

Marc stared at her thoughtfully. Then he pushed his chair back and stood.

Chapter Twelve

Early Friday morning, Libby left Enzo toiling in the house. As she headed up the hill toward Vivia's, she enjoyed the relief that everything had ended on a positive note with Marc the night before. It had taken a serious turn there for a few minutes with all the talk of grandparents, bad blood, and broken hearts. Before he had stepped back into the rain, she had stepped into his arms. With her voice deliberately light, and her kisses coaxing, she reminded him that since there were no marriages pending, the families had nothing to concern themselves with. "Unless of course you know something I don't about Vivia and Enzo." That had made him smile. Their kiss good night had been deep and sweet, leaving her wanting more.

This evening held promise. She was going to Marc's home for dinner and she'd be sure to steer all conversation away from sore spots. After all, she and Marc couldn't be expected to fix what had taken years to disassemble.

The sun was brilliant, the kind of day she remembered from her childhood. It screamed summer vacation and she heard the children's laughter before she came upon them. A spirited game of soccer was taking place on the paved area in front of the bakery's loading dock. One of the boys saw Libby and, with a rascal's smile, aimed a kick in her direction. Laughing, she skipped sideways a few steps to intersect the rolling ball, and attempted to boot it back to the boy. He grinned at her and ran to fetch it. Two women lingered nearby, watching over the children. Libby gathered her courage and called to them in Italian.

"Buon giorno. Fa bel tempo." Good day, it's beautiful out.

"Buon giorno. Sì, un perfetto oggi per un gioco di calcio. In bocca al lupo."

"Ciao."

"Ciao."

She smiled as if she understood, and continued the rest of the way silently repeating the words.

Vivia's door stood open. *"Ciao,* Viv. Thanks for shopping with me."

"I come, Libby." Vivia appeared a moment later, still fiddling with the strap of her purse.

"Do you want to take my car?" Libby asked.

"No, I should drive." Vivia closed her door, but didn't lock it.

"There are some children at the bakery. One of the women with them said, *'In bocca al lupo.'* I hear, mouth and wolf."

"*Sì*, it is a saying. In the mouth of the wolf. It means good luck. They practice now and will play the game later." Vivia used her hands to punctuate the present and then, sweeping them forward, indicated the future.

"Your English has improved over the last couple of months." Libby admired Vivia openly. The Italian woman had conveyed a complicated series of tenses with that one simple thought.

Vivia, bright with the compliment, gave her a little nudge with her elbow. "Your Italian has improved since May." They grinned.

"Have you ever gone to the opera in Verona?" Libby asked as she slid into Vivia's passenger seat and pulled the belt on.

"When I was a child. With the school."

"Did people dress up? Wear long gowns?"

"Some dress up. Some do not. Why?"

"I'm going to the opera. That's why I want to go to Trieste today, to buy something to wear."

Vivia didn't say anything, but Libby could feel tension emanating from her. Apparently, she suspected that Libby would be going with Marc. They rounded a curve and started a straightaway where the road widened to allow cars to pull over and admire the view.

"I'm thinking I'd like a dress," Libby continued. "Long, at least calf length, fancy. Something sexy and swishy."

"Swishy?"

Libby pantomimed a flowing dance with her hands. They chatted easily about clothing and fashion, passing fields separated every few moments by scatterings of stone houses, car dealerships, restaurants, and churches.

As Vivia turned confidently toward the autostrade, Libby braced herself for a hair-raising race in the Italian traffic. But Vivia drove more sedately than Marc so that by the time they took an off-ramp, she had grown almost used to darting in and out between huge transfer trucks and tiny cars. Now they traveled along a coastal road past busy beaches where people lounged around cement platforms overlooking narrow strips of gravel or sand. At the approach to Trieste, things got hair-raising again.

"I'm so glad you're driving," Libby said. She attempted to read the street names and compare them to the map opened on her lap. Apparently, small red-and-white bull's-eye signs directed one to the center of the city, but sometimes the streets seemed to suddenly end, or shrink into one lane, or split into three.

"It is not big," Vivia replied, "but very busy. We will park near to the water. Is expensive but easy."

The Gulf of Trieste sparkled on the right, and a line of large, marble-looking façades faced them across the wide boulevard on the left. Even with her sunglasses on, Libby shaded her eyes with her hand. Everything glistened white.

"It's very lovely. But the buildings are so different

than those I've seen elsewhere in Italy." The architecture was much more solid, somber, and less ornate, but with beautiful lines and a strong sense of balance.

"*Sì*, Austrian."

In her mind's eye, Libby pictured a present-day map of Europe. Austria was far to the north. Her confusion must have shown. Vivia took her by the elbow and led her down the sidewalk, all the while giving a history lesson partly in Italian, and partly in English.

"So," Libby said, counting off with her fingers. "This city has been Austrian, Italian, German, Yugoslavian, Roman, Goth . . . oh, and French." She'd missed some of the names.

"Founded by the Illyrians."

Libby rolled her eyes and laughed. She remembered that Marc had given her a similar history lesson as they stood on the top of the mountain. Here, in this relatively small geographic space, so many cultures fit together like pieces of a puzzle, and yet each group struggled—sometimes fought—to maintain its distinct ethnic personality. The Loszachs and the Iacomes were a miniscule segment of the same larger picture.

They walked along the seaside admiring the swanky yachts tied nearby, then headed inland, up one side of a wide canal. Luckily, Vivia knew the lay of the land so Libby was able to soak in the sights without fear of getting lost. Away from the water, cars were parked everywhere, up over the curbs and squeezed into tiny corners. Motorcycles leaned against walls. Police in white helmets strolled in pairs as if they didn't have a worry in the world. Modern-looking apartments with narrow balconies faced ornate, centuries-old buildings.

The shops ranged from tourist haunts to out-of-reach expensive. Just before the stores closed for siesta, Libby chose a black silk dress with a brocade top that came with a matching shawl.

"This," Vivia said, pointing to the flowing fabric of the skirt, "is sweeshy."

Libby chuckled. "I can wear it to Christmas parties back home." She stopped primping in front of a mirror when the thought of going back home cast a shadow over her mood. Suddenly Christmas parties didn't hold any appeal. In fact, the future looked lonely. She would miss Vivia, Croce, and—Marc. She returned to the changing room.

"We eat lunch now?" Vivia asked through the louvered door.

"Yes, please. I'm starving."

"Outdoors at a café? Or indoors?"

"Outdoors."

They chose a table under a colorful café umbrella. Across the square stood a spectacular church with a half-dozen shiny blue dome roofs. "I have to come back to Trieste someday," Libby said wistfully. "That church is breathtaking and I don't have time today to go inside."

"There are castles and churches and much to see."

"Yes. And I will make the time to see it all but not today. Are you sure you don't mind stopping by the hardware store?" Libby accepted a menu from a waiter wearing a white apron around his waist and nodded her thanks.

"No, I don't mind. There is one on the way." Vivia's voice became dramatic. "But Cousin Libby, all you know is the hardware store. You are not a tourist."

Libby chuckled. "I'll come back someday as one."

"You should move here."

Libby looked about the square thoughtfully. Everything felt so foreign and exotic. "I don't even speak the language."

"You have been here months only, and you speak many words."

"Not well enough to find a job."

"Then you teach the English."

"English as a second language." The idea had merit. She didn't need to be fluent in Italian to teach English. But how would she live while she hunted for a teaching job? She couldn't simply live with relatives; most of them lived in the village. She'd need to live where there were English-language schools. What savings she'd managed would be severely depleted after this trip. She glanced down at the bags leaning on the legs of her chair. Oh well, she'd save that particular problem for another day.

"You would miss your home?" Vivia asked.

Libby nodded. "I have a good job, friends, a nice place to live. And my brother and my parents live there."

"Do you miss them?"

"Not too much. We speak on the phone and I send e-mails. So far I've been very busy restoring the house and . . . things." And being with Marc.

"Libby," Vivia said quietly. "I would be very happy if you moved to Croce. But you must not think Marc Iacome would be happy."

Libby felt stung. She almost pulled away when Vivia reached across and squeezed her hand. On reflection, she thought that perhaps her cousin was right. How would Marc feel? Trapped? Pressured? The notion made her sad. Why couldn't two single, unattached adults simply fall in love? Love? She shook her head at the thought and turned her attention to the waiter.

Even though her appetite had disappeared, Libby randomly chose a pizza from the long list, and asked for an iced coffee. He wrote down Vivia's choice and wandered off.

"This, ah, friendship with Marc, it is hard for you?"

"Oh, Vivia. It's wonderful, and no—it's not hard. Just the families make it difficult."

"I wish to say, Libby, I worry for you." Vivia placed her hand over her heart.

She smiled softly at her cousin's kind intentions. "I do too."

Marc loved his mother. Normally, he enjoyed her company too. In typical mother fashion, she fussed over him, worried that he needed to eat better, nagged at him to get a haircut, and sighed that deep mother's sigh that he needed find a good girl and get married. And normally, he took it all in good grace. But not today. Today, he wanted her to clear out of his house. Now.

"That smells heavenly. You have a lady friend coming over, Marcello?" She lifted the top of the pot bubbling on the stove and smelled. "You checked the seasonings? You never put in enough garlic. Here, give me a spoon, I'll fix it for you."

"It's fine, Madre."

"What kind of wine are you serving?"

He put both his hands on his mother's shoulders and turned her toward him. "You know I love you." He kissed her cheek. "Now leave."

Her shoulders deflated. "Oh, Marcello? Why won't you let me meet this new girl of yours? I see a new girl there in your eyes. Am I not good enough?"

"No one is good enough for you." He took her elbow and started back toward the foyer and the door.

"At least tell me her name."

"No, Madre." They paused there while he took her sweater—cashmere, by the feel of it—from the closet and draped it over her narrow, square shoulders. She removed her car keys from the copper catchall by his door.

Anna Iacome had parked her compact Mercedes between his muddy truck and the red Ferrari. Just as Marc encouraged his mother out the door, Libby pulled up behind the truck. She'd already stepped from her vehicle before she saw them. Even from above her, Marc could see the wince flash across her face when she recognized his mother. He knew the two had seen each other at the bonfire, although neither had mentioned it. Libby recovered quickly, smiled, and waved.

"This is your female friend, Marcello? This woman?" Anna hissed through the side of her mouth. She didn't smile.

"Now you know why I wanted you to leave."

"It hurts me that you would do this."

With a disapproving shake of his head, he whispered, "If she were anyone else but Mattia's granddaughter . . ."

"Exactly." She lifted her chin and started down the stairs.

Libby slammed the car door, hitched her bag higher on her shoulder, and strolled to meet them. She carried a large bouquet of exotic flowers in her arms.

"Libby, this is my mother, Anna Iacome." He nudged his mother forward.

"*Buona sera*," she said, smiling. "*Mi chiamo* Libby Zufferlia."

Anna eyed the brilliant bouquet. She looked as if she were about to comment on them, but instead said merely, "How do you do?" Anna spoke in clear English and, as though her upbringing dictated it, offered Libby a limp handshake.

Marc rolled his eyes at Libby before accompanying his mother to her car. As he opened the door for her, she said, "We will talk about this in the morning."

"Yes, we will." His tone held affection but said clearly that he would brook no nonsense. He raised his hand in a wave as his mother drove away.

"She's very beautiful, your mother," Libby said.

"She is." He gave her an apologetic smile. "Sorry about that."

"No, I'm sorry I didn't call before coming. I even had the cell phone with me, but I just didn't think of it."

"You and your *telefonino*. Hopeless."

She passed the flowers to him. "Normally I'd bring wine to a dinner invitation, but . . . wine to an Iacome? It's like bringing coal to Newcastle. I think not." She smiled but it didn't reach her eyes.

Clearly she was still dismayed by the unwelcome reception she had received, but Marc appreciated the fact that, at least outwardly, she tried to make light of the situation. "Let's go put these in water."

As Marc ushered her into his home, he watched Libby's face. For some unfathomable reason, he'd been afraid that she'd feel indifferent about it. Not so. She sighed complimentary comments every couple of steps, admiring the open staircase with the mezzanine above, the two-story-high picture windows overlooking a vista that stretched, on a clear day, as far as Venice.

When they reached the dining area, she jerked to a stop and flattened her hand on her heart. "I think I've died and gone to heaven."

"You like it?" he asked, needlessly.

"Wow." She ran a hand over the polished surface of the table, then pointed at each chair, counting. "You can seat a couple dozen people here."

"We, my family, we needed a big room to eat in."

When she turned to him, her eyes were large and shiny, perhaps even a little sad. "You do that a lot?"

"The house hasn't been finished very long, but I think

that soon we will hold the big meals here: birthdays, Christmas, Easter."

"And do you do the cooking?"

He threw his head back and laughed. "You just met her," he said meaningfully, "and my mother is a sweet pussycat compared to my aunts." He opened his arms wide to include the dining room and adjoining kitchen. "No, I think I'll leave the food to them. This space is my contribution to the meal."

Now she gazed up at the windows. "This is an entirely different view than from the front, but just as spectacular."

Marc had to agree. The room faced the side of the mountain, so he could see forested hills and alpine meadows climbing up and up. The green was bright in the foreground but dimmed with each progressive layer to end up a mossy gray in the distance.

He watched while Libby, gazing out the window, made her way back toward the cooking area. When she turned her attention to that room, she staggered to a stop and cried, "Oh, God is in heaven, and all's right with the world."

Her reaction thrilled him. He threw back his head and howled with laughter. All the years of dreaming about what kind of house he wanted to live in, the months poring over architectural designs, then the careful selection of materials, appliances, fixtures, and the building, all that time, he'd pictured a moment just like this.

Libby ran her hand over the marble counter laid out

with two place settings with a candle between them. A bottle of wine was decanted and strains of soft music whispered.

"I hope you don't mind. I thought this would be more intimate than the dining room. You can keep me company as I make the salad." He poured her a glass of wine and she slid comfortably onto a barstool.

"This is *perfetto.*"

He had gone a little crazy the day he ordered his supplies. He knew perfectly well that every accoutrement known to mankind was in this kitchen. Marc would either have to become a fabulous cook or he'd have to have high hopes in a mate. The thought settled somewhere in his belly. It was then that he realized she had spoken.

"What's for dinner?" Libby repeated. She must have seen his mind wander but didn't press the issue.

"We're having the bachelor special."

At the same time, they chimed, "Spaghetti."

He reached for a large wooden salad bowl and began rubbing the sides with garlic. With deft hands, he cracked an egg, added a dash of this and a pinch of that, grabbed a whisk and went to work on the dressing. "We will continue the tour after dinner, if you like."

"I like." She turned the stool around and appraised all she could see. "You have exquisite taste. Everything has such clean lines, beautiful, rich colors, nothing left to chance. You must be so pleased with your home."

He nodded. His pleasure doubled in watching her.

He strained the pasta, ladled a healthy portion of

thick sauce, lifted the Caesar salad into the bowls, and eased onto the stool beside her. She topped off their wineglasses and held hers aloft. "Cheers."

"Cin cin." He touched his to hers.

He felt her leg brush against his as they began their meal. Proximity. Marc congratulated himself on his decision to eat in the kitchen.

As they ate, they laughed at uncooperative pieces of spaghetti, made plans for the trip to Verona, spoke of the opera, and Libby chatted about her trip to Trieste. They were sliding back their dishes and touching their lips with their napkins before he realized it. Time just flew by when he was with her. Had he ever felt so comfortable with a woman before? So attracted to a woman before? He shook his head as he put a pot of coffee on.

"I'm ready to see the rest of your house." She took the mug in both hands as she spoke. Her eyes twinkled. "It's so big that the walk will do me good."

He first showed her a work-in-progress he called the conservatory. By now, the sun had set so the windows reflected only the near-empty interior. "Is this the south exposure?" she asked. Her voice echoed off the glass walls and ceiling and raw cement floor.

He nodded. "I'll work on this in the winter, before the pruning season begins."

"Will you use it as a greenhouse?" she asked, sounding faintly breathless at the prospect.

"No, I'm not much for gardening." He chuckled, then added, "My mother wants to put plants in here, but I told her to build her own conservatory."

"What's it for then?"

"Perhaps a lap pool. Maybe a hot tub. I haven't decided. What do you think?"

"Do you like to swim laps?"

He lifted a shoulder in a shrug. "I need some kind of exercise in the off season."

"Will it steam up the windows?"

He gave it a moment's thought. "I don't know. There must be something to prevent that, yes?"

"I'm sure there is. Is there a room nearby where you can change into a bathing suit?"

"I'll just change here. No one can see me through the windows, unless they're walking in the forest or have a telescope."

"Your guests might not feel the same way." She smiled.

He had a sudden image of her emerging from the pool, hair slick to her head, wearing only something tiny and black. Now, that would steam up the windows. Yes, he thought, a lap pool.

"What colors are you thinking of using for tiles and wall paint?" she asked.

"I don't know," he said, dragging his mind back to the topic. "Do you think it should match the kitchen?"

"Coordinate, at least. And you'd have to have plants in here. I agree with your mother on that."

As they discussed the possibilities, Marc began to see the room as it could be. He pictured the two of them side by side, floating on their backs near the window, with the view of the mountain towering overhead. The image had his blood pounding.

"Your house is stunning, Marc. Just wonderful."

"Thank you," he managed through his dry mouth. He cleared his throat and took a sip of the coffee he had all but forgotten. "It's still empty though."

She nodded. "You'll have fun picking out paintings and furniture and rugs and . . . everything."

He stepped closer and tucked a strand of hair back behind her ear. "I wish you could stay and help me decorate it."

She looked at him, as if judging whether or not he was serious. Was he? he asked himself. He pictured the volcano of emotions that would erupt in his own family and veered from that particular train of thought.

Chapter Thirteen

Nothing marked the passage of time in a little village the size of Croce like special events. The village was abuzz with plans for the huge flea market scheduled for Saturday. Organizers had their heads full of which table went where and which booth was beside which stall. Striking a balance of keeping similar products close but not too close was their main concern. Some held to the theory that competition was good for business while the others felt that each row should represent the caliber of the market and offer as wide a selection as possible.

Libby had prepared a list of bargains to hunt for and each day she seemed to add another item to her wish list. Like the days leading up to the Feast of St. John the Baptist at the summer solstice, Libby heard talk of little else.

Libby went to bed in a sleepy little village and woke to a transformed Croce. Vendors had set up their stalls before dawn. Tables now packed the field where the summer solstice festival had been held. With the field as the hub, stalls radiated from there up streets and alleys. The loading dock in front of the Loszach Bakery became an orderly parking lot, but by full morning, cars overflowed up and down the main road leading to the valley. Libby eyed a few of the cars suspiciously and was eternally hopeful they had emergency brakes on.

From where she and Vivia stood on the street above, the field looked like a caravan of canvas roofs. The air, typically sweet from the bakery, now carried a slew of new and different aromas: coffee and cheese, soaps and candles. It was Libby's strategy to do a quick walk-through before buying anything. Vivia's approach was to "take no prisoners." If she liked it, needed it, or simply wanted it, she would own it. They decided to take their own routes and meet later for a bite of lunch.

The festive atmosphere was contagious and Libby found herself smiling at faces, new and familiar, as she began to weave through the marketplace. It seemed with every passing step she was embracing an aunt or uncle or kissing a cousin. Even Aunt Erika was there, swinging her cane to clear a path, enjoying herself enormously.

Half a dozen booths carried inexpensive clothes that waved back and forth on their wire hangers. There were tables of bric-a-brac next to expensive antique furniture, dusty books next to church vestments. It was easy to see which school of thought the organizers had settled on.

At midmorning, Libby trotted back to the house to unload her purchases: two well-made lamps, a pile of color-coordinated bath towels and mats, two straw hats she couldn't resist, and a rattling sack of kitchen implements. She was having so much fun that she simply unlocked the door, dumped the bags and lamps in the kitchen, and then headed out again.

On the way back down to the market she came upon Melena with two of her children, Lisa trudging along behind her carrying the purchases and Carmela swinging her little legs happily in her stroller. Libby bent to kiss the top of their heads and exchange such pleasantries with Melena as their language limitations allowed. Libby walked with them for a block, then veered off. She'd seen Marc, accompanied by his mother, picking over a long table full of soldiers' medals, swords, and firearms. It was instinct more than common sense that had her moving his way. When she caught his eye, Marc smiled but his mother studiously ignored her.

"You have no parcels, Libby?" he asked in all innocence as his fingers played with hers behind a showcase.

"Good morning, Mrs. Iacome." Good manners prevailed.

Marc's mother's head gave an almost imperceptible nod but she didn't look Libby's way. To Marc, Libby answered, "I've already taken them home." Keeping her voice as light as possible, she arched a brow, warning him to behave.

He turned to show her that he carried a backpack. "My mother uses me as a mule." At that, Anna shot Marc a sharp look, but he simply bounced a teasing eyebrow toward her. She poked him in the side with her elbow, hiding a smile. Clearly, she couldn't resist his charm. *Well, the two of us have more in common than you know,* Libby thought. Her eyes took in Marc, all tanned, tall, handsome, and playful. *Oh my.*

"My cousin Enzo is my aunt Marana's pack animal."

He made a slight go-to motion with his head toward Enzo. Libby checked that Anna wasn't watching, then pointed an unobtrusive finger toward herself, her expression a question, then at Enzo. Marc winked at her.

One part of Libby enjoyed this secret communication between them. It was exciting and taboo. It took her mind where it perhaps shouldn't be headed, in public on a Saturday morning. Yes, it made her blood race. The other part of her, the sensible, sensitive part, felt it deceitful and juvenile. She knew that every fiber of her being wanted to go around to the other side of the table and link her arm into his. How lovely it would feel to have him snuggling her closer to his side. The other day, she had daydreamed about meeting him there, in the market, but reality was very different. Her heart sighed. Perhaps it had always been so.

Croce, 1948

Mattia hurried along behind her mother down the steep hill toward the market. They smiled and waved at friends, and stared at the strangers from the valley who had come to Croce for the annual market. From above, the caravans looked bright and cheerful with their flags fluttering and canvas bright in the sun. They were shabbier up close, she remembered from the previous year. The war had been hard on the Gypsies.

It had rained the night before so once they left the stones the ground was soft and slippery underfoot. Mattia shifted her empty basket to her other side and hooked her arm through her mother's. The horses, both those belonging to the vendors and those belonging to the people who had ridden over from other villages, had been tethered all around the edge of the fairgrounds. The air smelled pungent with their droppings. Whenever a car appeared the village children ran toward it, their voices an excited babble.

Her parents were always talking about how things were getting back to normal, but Mattia didn't really remember much about life before the war. She had her friends and her school and, of course, Leo.

They spent the next hour wandering around the tables and tents, picking up an almost-new beater from one place, a skein of wool at another. Then Mattia saw Sophia in the distance. She left her mother and made her way through the crowd toward her friend.

"Hello, Sophia," she said.

"Hello." Sophia didn't look her in the eye.

"Do you feel well? You're awfully pale."

Sophia shrugged. "I have to find my mother."

Before she could leave, Mattia grabbed her arm. "Please don't be like that. Tell me what I did wrong."

"You know what you did," Sophia hissed.

"No, I don't. I have no idea why you're angry with me."

Now Sophia looked at her. "You embarrassed me when I was with my . . . friends."

Mattia tensed: They were standing in the middle of a busy market day where anyone could overhear them. She looked around and saw that girl from the vineyard, Deborah, watching them.

"Let's go talk about it." Mattia pulled Sophia's arm.

"I don't want to."

"Please, Sophia. I'm going to have it out with you. Do you want me to do it here?" She tilted her head toward Deborah.

Sophia sighed heavily and trod toward the edge of the field. Her looks had changed. The white blouse that she had worn comfortably a few months earlier was too small. The buttons strained so that Mattia could see her undergarment through the gaps. Her beautiful, lively face now looked drawn and thin. Even her long black hair, a feature she'd normally be proud of, hung lank and dirty.

The boulders that had been cleared from the field decades earlier were piled in a long row at the edge of the field. Trying to be unobtrusive, Mattia looked down the line of trees to see if Leo had left her a signal that he wanted her to go to her secret meeting place. She couldn't see anything, but from this angle it was difficult to tell. What was she doing thinking of Leo now, when her friend was obviously hurting. They sat on the rocks.

"Please tell me what's wrong."

Sophia sighed and shook her head. Her eyes filled with tears.

"Have you fallen in love?"

"I . . . thought I had."

"Is he still here?" Mattia looked around. Would she recognize an American if he wandered amid the crowd? One with Italian heritage? One who spoke Italian even? Even though the war was long over, feelings were still too raw in the village. Everyone had a friend or family member killed in the war. Mattia herself had seen dead men. She remembered one time when the women brought back a man they'd found in the forest. It was wintertime and he wore a white feather-filled camouflage suit. A blossom of red blood stood stark against the wool all across his midsection. The man, it turned out, came from Udine. His unit had been ambushed in the mountains and he'd been left behind. The women tended to him, and sent word to his family, but he died anyway.

An American soldier would not be safe here, even now.

"He's back in Trieste. He doesn't come here anymore."

Mattia wanted to hug her friend, but their relationship was too tentative these days. Instead she pulled her hands into her lap. "He hurt you," she stated.

"He doesn't know."

"That he hurt you?"

"That I'm pregnant."

Croce, present day

Libby wove her way around the tables and through the packs of people to stand next to Enzo. His eyes lit up. Then he looked around to see whether or not anyone watched.

"This is for you. For the house," he said in slow, accented English. He nudged a parcel wrapped in brown paper toward her.

It felt heavy and clanked when she lifted it. "*Grazie*, Enzo." Her fingers rested on his wrist for a moment in silent appreciation. He had become a friend.

He shrugged, but blushed. "*Prego*. But it is from Marc." He looked abashed.

"Libby! Libby!" A woman's excited voice rang above the buzzing market.

She couldn't see who had called. A couple of local people stared at her, eyes wide.

"Libby! Come, Libby!"

Marc came striding through the crowd. "It's your cousin, Vivia."

"Viv? Something must be wrong." It was so unlike Vivia to raise her voice without good reason. With her heart pounding, Libby took off toward her. Marc and Enzo followed.

They found Vivia at the edge of the market, on the incline overlooking the field, her eyes wide. "Mattia Zufferlia, Libby."

At the mention of her grandmother's name, Libby froze, fearing that something awful had happened to her.

"Look!" Vivia was saying.

Libby followed Vivia's pointed finger. There her grandmother stood on the street, paying a taxi driver. With a yelp, Libby galloped up the hill.

"Nonna! Nonna, you're here!" They came together in a bear hug, kisses flying. "You sneaky thing, you."

Word traveled like wildfire and mere seconds later, the street thronged with Loszach family members and old friends of Mattia's, all talking in a blur of Italian.

Libby stood aside, her heart warmed at the enthusiasm of the welcome her grandmother received and the myriad of smacking cheek kisses. The poor taxi driver, who had given up trying to inch his car through the crowd, leaned out his window talking to people.

Suddenly, Libby became aware that the voices behind her weren't so jolly. She swung around to see the Iacome family, men, women, and children, had gathered on the other side of the lane with the forest of market stalls behind them. Anna, Marana, and another woman appeared to be holding Leopoldo back from going toward Mattia. Libby could only pick out a word here and there amid the angry babble. She had learned a fine glossary of swear words listening to the workmen during construction and from what she caught wind of here, none of what the Iacomes said sounded flattering to Nonna. Libby's mouth dropped open, aghast.

The silence that fell among the Loszach group as they heard the exchange among the other family was momentary. Suddenly, a hue and cry went up as all began to talk at once, speaking louder and more emphatically with each word. Drago shouted toward the other family and, taking his lead, the other Loszachs directed their anger across the lane.

The Iacomes responded in kind.

Libby stared in disbelief, her head going from the Iacomes to the Loszachs and back. Something large and cold and very bitter settled in the pit of Libby's stomach.

Could this feud lead to violence?

Tears scalded Libby's eyes and a pressure burned in her throat. Through her tears, she looked to Marc. There he was, taller than the rest, standing on the other side of the narrow lane with Enzo and others she couldn't name. All around him, just as around her, voices raised and hands gesticulated, punctuating every word, every sentence. Marc looked furious.

Chapter Fourteen

Ordinary people who lived and worked in the same community, people who only minutes ago had picked their way around a much-celebrated flea market, shopping, eating, laughing, now stood separated by a lane. Separated by an age-old conflict. Separated by distrust, dislike, and dissension.

Out of the cacophony, one voice raised above all others.

"Basta!" Leopoldo Iacome, the patriarch of the Iacome family, roared. The gaggle around him stilled. He eyed them sternly and the women stepped back. He moved away from his family.

Across the narrow lane, Mattia Zufferlia raised her chin and stepped through her family, her eyes on Leopoldo, tall, silver, and handsome. Mattia, graceful and dignified, had never looked more beautiful to Libby than she did at this moment. The fire in her grand-mother's eyes spoke of a flame tamped for a half century. She looked over at Leo, then did a slow examination of the people, the market, and, or so it seemed to Libby, the trees surrounding the field. Then she gave Leopoldo a strange look, a questioning eyebrow raised.

Silence fell as it does, in a cascade, stages of aware-ness reaching each in its own time. The man and woman stopped, one on either side of the cobblestone roadway.

"The tree is gone, Leo," she said in English.

"Long gone," he replied, his voice harsh with anger or accusation.

"Did it die a natural death?"

"I chopped it out by the roots. I burned the wood and the rope."

Mattia reacted as if he'd slapped her. Libby felt angry and defensive. She sprang to get between her grand-mother and the angry patriarch.

"You shouldn't have come back, Mattia," Leopoldo snapped.

"Leo?"

Obviously Leopoldo was hurting her grandmother somehow. Libby took Mattia's arm. It trembled under her touch. "Come and see what I've done to the house, Nonna."

But Mattia wouldn't be so easily deflected. She kept staring at Leopoldo. "You were such a kind boy."

The sorrow in her voice had Libby glaring at Leopoldo. Before she had a chance to say anything her great uncle, Gerardo, was there. He kissed Mattia gravely on both cheeks. Mattia took a deep breath and then greeted him warmly.

Gerardo spoke to her in a quiet voice, then led her to the taxi still idling on the street. They both got into the backseat. The people cleared a path for the vehicle and it moved off. Stunned, Libby followed it with her eyes until it turned out of sight.

Libby now swung to the crowd, the mob. Her hands were still clenched in fists.

Leopoldo stared after the taxi for a moment, then turned and marched back down the road the other way. Anna and Marana scurried to catch up to him. When Libby realized that Marc was coming to join her, she tensed again. "What was that about?" she demanded of him.

"She hurt him badly."

"*She* hurt *him!*"

He lifted his chin. "But of course."

"There are two sides to every story." Libby fought to keep her voice level but inside she seethed. To think that someone could take that man, that Leopoldo Iacome's side against Mattia was inconceivable.

The Loszach family, Drago and Melena, Vivia, Victor and Natale, and the children herded Libby up to the house. Apparently there would be an impromptu family meeting. Their voices buzzed around her but Libby didn't even try to translate the words. Her heart ached and she didn't know exactly why.

Besides the crew of workmen, Libby had never had more than a few people visiting at one time. Momentarily she felt overwhelmed at the hubbub. She regretted that she had dumped her parcels on the floor earlier and gathered them up into a tidy pile. Then she remembered her duties as hostess. Coffee. The coffee she usually made, she knew, wouldn't be up to the Croce high standards, so she ground and scooped several more tablespoons for the pot. This would be so strong a spoon would stand up in it or be disintegrated trying. And tea. For the more faint of heart, like herself, she put the kettle on. Melena and Vivia were by her side, each lifting the purchases of food from the market from their bags. They set about cutting bread, salami, fruit, and cheese. In celebration, in discord, Italians ate.

"You have grappa?" Drago asked. He kept clenching and unclenching his fists.

She nodded toward the cupboard where the doors still didn't fit properly. He yanked on it so that the slat wood flap slapped against the wall. The men took their glasses and the bottle of grappa and crowded into the sitting room while the women looked around the house. Their voices carried, the men's rising and falling in discussion of Mattia and Leopoldo and the women's from beyond the sitting room where they were inspecting the new bathroom. Even though Libby understood only a few words here and there, their approval made her proud. She felt her racing pulse begin to slow.

"We look upstairs?" Vivia asked, poking her head back into the kitchen.

"Yes. Will you take these lamps for the room on the

second floor—for beside Nonna's bed? You'll know it when you see it."

Vivia, lamps in hand, disappeared. Libby sighed. Vivia was a good friend. Her footsteps echoed with the others as the women and children hurried up the new staircase. Once up there, their feet made scuffling sounds through the ceiling. Libby stared up, wondering if dry-wall dust would come sprinkling down as it had when the construction was underway. It didn't. She continued with her food preparations.

Libby suspected that the men would bluster and the women would ignore what had happened not an hour ago on the village street. That seemed to be the way and so she tried to put the incident aside in her mind. At least Nonna was safe with Gerardo. Alone in the kitchen amid a full house, she laid out a tray. Plates, napkins, mugs, cream, and milk. The food she'd leave as it was on the heavy wooden cutting board. Everyone could help them-selves. It was not a time for ceremony. This was family.

She thought about her preparation for Nonna and was glad she'd painted her room in plenty of time so that all traces of the strong scent were gone. And that she had al-ready washed the new sheets. The bed smelled sunshine fresh. And the new lamps would add a warmth to the pretty bedroom, as well as a reading light. Nonna was a voracious reader.

Suddenly, she stopped. Now that Nonna had arrived, it would be time for her to leave Italia. She sank onto a chair, gravity pulling hard at her. She rested her head in her hands. Through a dull throb that marked the beginning of a headache, she thought about going home. Her mind pictured her small, sunny condominium, its art, and its plants. Her home. Her contract at the college had been extended but even so, she wouldn't begin teaching for another few weeks; there was still time for that road trip she'd planned to take with her girlfriend back home. That should be a happy thought. Shouldn't it? Then why did tears threaten? Her face buried deeper into her hands.

Home. It seemed like a lifetime ago. It was a different life there. An easy, uncomplicated life. Not this Italian life, full of secrets, confrontation, family—with its foreboding Croce definition of family.

And Marc. At the thought of him, she moaned. She loved him so deeply. That was the heart of the matter. She was in love. She pressed a hand over her heart and let a few tears fall. Just a few, she promised herself, to loosen this heavy ache. Her mind's eye saw Marc as he had looked the first day. His hair, his eyes, his lips, smiling as she had tried to ease herself, unobtrusively, over the gate of the wrong house. She smiled at the memory. More tears fell.

Libby tried to collect herself now while she was alone. Taking deep breaths she went to the sink to splash cold water onto her face. She turned, reaching for the towel, and there stood Vivia and Melena. Libby knew there was no disguising the fact that she had been crying, so she just gave in to it. As tears streamed her face, the two women, her family, stepped forward and enclosed her in their arms. Nothing was said, no words spoken, no explanation necessary. Just comfort and understanding were offered and Libby accepted.

The storm of emotion passed and, as is so often the case, people eased the tension with laughter. It was the release, or embarrassment, or pure relief that it was over. Whatever the reason, the women gave one another one last squeeze and set about serving the food.

She and Marc had said they had to enjoy their time together and not think of the future. Right, she told herself with resolve. She could do that. She had to. In fact, this should be a time of happy anticipation: She and Marc planned to head out to Verona and the opera in the morning.

Should she still go? Could she leave Nonna alone her first night in Croce? She thought about the people milling about the house. Of course she could leave her grandmother in the care of her own family.

In the sitting room most of the bottle of grappa was gone and the men were still in a dark mood.

"Why did you not tell us Mattia was coming today?" Drago demanded.

"I didn't know."

"You must know why she decided to move back here." He narrowed his eyes at her. "Was it because of Leopoldo Iacome?"

"How could you ask that? You saw the way he treated her," she said, her own voice sharp. "And I don't appreciate your tone."

"Then why? Why did she send you here to spend all

the money on *this*?" He waved a dismissive hand at the house.

Insulted to the core, Libby set the tray firmly on a stool. Keeping her answers in simple language and keeping her temper in check, Libby stated, "Croce is her home. Her husband died. She wants to come home. Is that so hard to understand?"

"Yes. She did not discuss this house or her plans with any of us before she sent you here."

Taking a deep breath, Libby passed around the coffee and motioned for everyone to help themselves. "Yes she did," she snapped. "How else do you suppose I got the key?"

Oh, she was tired. Bone weary. So much upheaval. So much talk. She eased herself onto the arm of the little sofa. "It is not for me to explain my grandmother's actions. She is a grown woman who knows her own mind." Remembering Mico's outburst at Uncle Gerardo's, she added, "Whatever plans you had for this house were your plans. Nonna knew nothing of it."

"Bah!" Drago barked.

Libby could feel her temper rising and the hammering in her head grew in response. She was no good at this and she knew she should make peace. At the very least, she should hold her tongue. Nothing good ever came when she let it loose.

"I don't know where you get off being angry about what she does to her own house!" Libby saw the way that her use of idiom confused him. "You have no say in what Nonna decides to do with her life."

Drago scoffed and then translated for the other men. She hated the way they were talking about her, looking at her, and the fact that she couldn't understand what they were saying.

"When I arrived here, this house was abandoned. It was filthy and left to rot all these years." Standing, she waved an arm around the home. "Now it is beautiful and now you want it. Well, you can't have it!"

Drago, one eyebrow raised, glanced round the room as if assessing what others had understood of her outburst. The confusion was as clear on his face as it was on the others'. Mico, who sat alone on the bottom step, stood and addressed the group in faster Italian than Libby could possibly have comprehended. The men all murmured and delivered scathing glances in Libby's direction. She rubbed at her temples, looking from one face to another. What did they have to be angry at her for? She didn't do anything wrong.

Then Libby thought about Marc and the way they'd been hiding their relationship. She had been deceitful. Now she understood why he had insisted on the secrecy. She flashed on his face as she'd last seen it. He hated her family. She felt the tears pushing against her eyeballs and pressed her fingernails into her own palms to try to stem the flow. It was no use. She turned away, sobbing.

It was Melena who put an end to it in a rush of Italian.

The men rose. Mico became shame-faced and was the first to head to the door. The men followed. Melena delivered an Italian directive to Vivia, where she lounged against the wall. She stood at attention.

Without a moment's notice Vivia had Libby by the elbow and led her through the kitchen to the outside staircase. Libby could hear Melena in the sitting room collecting dishes and ranting in Italian. She must have been half talking to herself because as Libby climbed the staircase, she could see the rest of the group heading along the lane. Mico and Lisa walked side by side, pushing Carmela in the stroller.

That morning when she felt something exciting would happen today, this wasn't what she had in mind.

Vivia steered Libby into her bedroom and walked briskly to the bed. She folded the covers down and eased Libby back, her protests and apologies falling on deaf ears. She was pulling the curtains closed as Melena entered the room with Libby's purse, a glass of water, and two aspirin. "Here. Take these. You rest." With the deftness gained only through motherhood, Melena eyed Libby until the pills were swallowed, brushed her hair off her forehead, and then smoothed the blankets around Libby's shoulders. "You sleep."

Libby slept.

Some hours later, her hand shot out from beneath the blanket to bat at a very persistent fly. Buzzing, endlessly buzzing. One eye opened and then the second. Her hand batted out again but no contact was made with the pest. She sat, fully dressed and glanced around. It was still light out—a slit of sunlight showed around the edge of the drapes. Of course, it was summer so it could be anytime before nine or so when the sun set. The buzzing. The fog began to clear as the wisps of sleep evaporated. Memory flooded. Libby touched her temples, frowning in concentration. No headache, just the full sinus that followed a crying jag. And the memory of tears of frustration and words of anger. Poor Drago. She'd find him and smooth things over. It had been a trying day and she was sure he would forgive her outburst.

When the droning began again reality informed her that it was her cellular phone and not a fly. Her eyes followed the sound and landed on her purse. Yes, Melena had carried it up with the pills. Rooting around, she clicked the little device open.

"Hello? *Pronto?*"

"*Cara.*" Marc's voice, gentle and quiet, was a balm. "You did not answer and I became worried. But for you not to answer should not worry me—you and the *telefonio* are not too familiar with each other." His laugh was smooth and pleasant. "But today was such a day."

Libby leaned back against her pillows, coaxing her mind to join the now. "What time is it? I've been sleeping."

"It is after dinner, half past eight. Are you all right? Are you ill?" His concern was evident as he rushed one sentence into the next. "Do you need me to come?"

How could he sound so normal? How could he not know that their relationship was forever changed by the way he had joined his family against hers?

"No, no, I am fine. It was just a headache. Too much—" She paused. What word could she use to downplay the afternoon? "Excitement." That would sum it up. "I am fine—really."

Call it shame at her own behavior or call it family loyalty, Libby felt reluctant to tell Marc of the family gathering. She needed to know what had gone through his mind earlier, but she wasn't ready to stir that emotion just yet.

Switching the little phone to her other ear, she smoothed her hair back into a ponytail and stood. "I am going to walk down to the kitchen for something to eat. I'll call you back in a little while. Okay?" She pocketed her phone, slipped on some shoes, and went outside and down the stairs.

A moment later, Libby entered the kitchen. Everything had been tidied up. She filled the kettle and wandered to the fridge. The cool air felt good on her hot skin so she stood there, staring into its interior. Nothing looked tempting. Her stomach felt too unsettled for food.

She decided to call Gerardo's house. The drive to Udine was long, but enough time had passed for them to reach home. They'd gone by taxi. Had anyone taken Gerardo's car back to his house? Just as she reached for her phone, it buzzed. She stared at the little viewing window and saw that it was Marc calling again. She closed her eyes and answered.

"I was wondering how you feel about Verona," he said. "Do you still want to go? Tell me honestly how you feel, Libby." She could hear a devilish tone creeping into his voice and she smiled as he went on in a rush. "It will break my heart if you say no, but I am a man . . . I can withstand the pain."

It suddenly occurred to Libby that Marc wasn't upset

at all and that perhaps he had no reason to be upset. Maybe his angry look earlier had been directed at what someone in the crowd had said and not at her nonna arriving. She felt giddy with relief.

"Yes, I want to go. I think I need to go away from this village for a while. I am looking forward to seeing the opera." Matching his devilish tone, she added huskily, "And being with you."

"Good answer. My heart lives to see another day. Then we will meet early in the bakery lot? Everything as before, as it was planned?"

"Yes. Marc? About today—"

He made a disgusted sound. "This place. It makes me crazy. But you and I, we are not affected, yes?"

He sounded so sincere she shook aside the last bit of suspicion. "We are not affected."

After they disconnected, Libby made a sandwich and tea to take to her balcony. She was virtually packed for the trip. She thought about the purchases she had made while shopping with Vivia in Trieste, and smiled. From the closet to her bag. That was it, all she had to do. She was humming her own rendition of a rock-and-roll song as she mounted the stairs once again.

Hot tea, tasty food, and a handsome, exotic man begging her to take a romantic holiday. Life was once again sweet. Her upset earlier was in reaction to the mob scene at the market, and to the way the men had treated her downstairs in the sitting room. It had nothing to do with Marc. Nothing at all.

Chapter Fifteen

Even before the opera began, Libby vibrated with excitement. She and Marc sat in the reserved area on the floor section of the Arena di Verona, in what promised to be a perfect location to watch the massive stage. The set for Verdi's Egyptian opera *Aida* towered above, at least sixty feet high, with thirty-foot golden statues of pharaohs in striding position on each side, and a pyramid-shaped backdrop.

Marc looked devastatingly handsome in his tuxedo: taller, broader in the shoulder, charming. It fit him perfectly and the fabric felt soft, like cashmere, under her fingers. She rubbed her cheek against his shoulder.

His eyes smiled at her. "You look lovely." He nuzzled closer. "And you smell nice."

She raised her chin and their lips met.

A vendor appeared with a tray of drinks and snacks,

so Marc purchased a couple bottles of water and two glasses of white wine. Libby had already been given a candle, which she laid on her lap to free her hands. In the excitement, her mouth had gone dry; she took care not to take more than a sip of the wine.

"It's so big," she said, craning her head to look around the arena. The people filling the seats farthest back looked like toys from this distance.

He followed her gaze. "They sit on stone benches up there."

"Stone? The original benches?" She hadn't thought that a two-thousand-year-old building would be used like this. In Canada, anything two hundred years old was considered historic, and was cherished and protected. "That must be hard on their backsides."

"You can rent a cushion. If it's been a sunny day you really need one, the stones are hot too."

"Not that you've ever sat in the nosebleed section."

"The what?" His momentary look of horror had her throwing back her head in laughter.

"It's an expression we use about the cheap seats—that they're so high there's a change in altitude. Get it? It's a joke. Altitude, nosebleed." She elbowed him. "You're supposed to laugh." She settled more comfortably in their first-rate seats. She was allowed to feel just a tad smug, wasn't she?

"Nosebleed section." He repeated it as though committing it to memory. Idiomatic expressions were the bane of language barriers. She remembered the wolf's mouth expression meaning good luck—go figure.

He reached into a pocket of his tuxedo for two sets of mini-binoculars and handed one to Libby. Opera glasses, no less. She didn't think they'd be necessary considering where they sat, unless she wanted to see the up-close expression on a performer's face.

By now, the sky shimmered above them as a deep, royal blue canopy of twilight chased the sun away. The talking and hum of movement settled. A hush fell. Anticipation. And then the conductor appeared on the stage. Thousands of people thundered applause. As the lights dimmed, the audience lit their candles. Marc chuckled at Libby's thrilled expression. Then he held her hand to still it so he could flick a light under the wick.

She gasped when the lights changed to an icy blue, not just on the soaring stage set, but on the entire arena.

From the moment the opera extravaganza began, her heart soared, her mind, mesmerized. The performers didn't use microphones, but she heard every note. It didn't matter that she didn't understand the words; she knew of what they sang. Her heart swelled. In the last scene, she cried genuine tears for the agony of the lovers on the stage.

When the lights came up and the crowd shuffled toward the exits, Libby remained seated, drained of strength. She looked at Marc. He cupped the back of her head, leaned forward, and kissed her on the forehead. Only then did she come to her senses.

"That was sensational," she breathed.

"It was."

Afterward, they wandered arm in arm down the streets

in a roundabout route toward their hotel, past darkened shop windows and quiet outdoor cafés. The pedestrian streets were wider here than in Venice although the same sort of ornately decorated, narrow balconies hung overhead. For the first time, Libby really understood what it meant to be walking on air; it felt as if her feet didn't touch the ground.

"Would you like to stop for a nightcap?" he asked.

She considered, and was about to dismiss the idea. She felt dreamy and uninhibited enough without adding alcohol to her blood. But she wanted to experience everything this evening. "Just one. I'm enjoying the walk and the evening air."

He chose a little café and they took their seats side by side so that they both could watch the world walk by. She ordered white wine and he grappa. They clinked their glasses together in a toast and he leaned in for a kiss. "Everything is perfect."

"It is, isn't it? That was so wonderful, Marc. Thank you very much for buying the tickets—for thinking of me."

He shifted in his seat. "You're welcome. I wanted to share this with you. I knew how you'd react."

Libby sipped her wine and, stretching her legs in front of her, rubbed a thigh against Marc's. It was a fantasy. Sitting there beside the man she loved, in an ancient city. What more could a woman ask? Everything was peaceful.

Then she tensed. Their grandparents. What was going on there? The evening before, Libby had spoken to her grandmother. She had sounded happy enough; had said she was glad to be back in Italia, happy to be with her family again. But under the words, Libby sensed a deep sadness.

"You look sad, Libby."

"Oh, I'm sorry, Marc. I was thinking about Nonna." She stopped and pulled her bottom lip between her teeth. "But I'll stop. I don't want to spoil the evening."

He looked pensive. "Is she at your house?"

"Her home," Libby corrected. "No, not tonight. She said she was going to visit in Udine for a day or two. I left a key with Vivia for when she gets back."

She opened her small shoulder bag and removed her phone. She had turned it off before entering the theater and with a click and snap, turned it on again. The little screen assured her that there were no missed calls. Holding the phone between her thumb and index finger, she pointedly dropped it into her purse.

"I don't know about you, Marc, but I don't want to think of our grandparents, Croce, family rifts—nothing tonight. Just this." She looked around appreciatively and then cocked an eyebrow at him. "Just us."

"Just us," he agreed. He held her chair as she rose and helped her adjust her shawl. Walking arm in arm they meandered toward the hotel.

Should she keep the phone on all night? No! This could be her last time alone with Marc and she made a solemn pledge to herself that she would enjoy the time to its fullest.

An arbored sidewalk followed the bank above the Adige River. Marc and Libby paused, elbows on the stone balustrade, and gazed down toward the Castelvecchio, ablaze with spotlights. Unusual battlements capped the castle walls—squares with V's sliced out of each center. It had been a scorching hot day, but the breeze off the water skimmed along her arms so she pulled her shawl up higher.

"Would you like my jacket?" Marc asked.

"That's sweet but no thank you. The cool is welcome. Oh, Marc, this is just all so stunningly beautiful."

He moved so her back nestled against his chest, and put both arms around her. When she leaned back, he pressed a kiss onto her hair. Her arms traced his, holding them in the simple embrace. Cars zoomed along a thoroughfare on the other side of the river but here, nestled in his arms, Libby felt safe, timeless, and content. Content? Even as the word sprang to her mind, she wondered.

"You will let me show you more of the city someday?"

Libby merely sighed. Her stay in Italy neared its end. She would return she knew, to visit Nonna, her cousins, but it would never be the same. But their lives would go on and she and Marc would see each other again as— what? Fond friends. Someone they knew when.

He would marry. Of course he would. She willed her breathing to slow. She knew going into this relationship that it could be nothing more than a summer fling. He had never led her on. If Nonna was a big girl, then so was she. The fact that she had fallen in love with him didn't come as a surprise. He was kind, caring, funny, loving— the list of his rare qualities had no end. And, just because he didn't return her love was no reason for recrimination.

She could find no fault with him on that score. Libby knew she couldn't make him love her in return. There was no formula, no demand, no argument to win his love.

Still in Marc's arms, Libby turned and looked into his eyes. "Yes, I would love to see all of Italia with you. Maybe someday." With a kiss, she took his arm and moved toward the hotel.

Alone in her room, Libby unzipped her garment bag, slid out her nightgown, and draped it on the bed. She eased out of her heels as she reached up to unpin her hair. Her fingers slid against her scalp and worked her hair loose. With a shake of her head, she let it fall where it wanted, fuller and wavier for the evening's restraint. Stepping out of her black silk outfit, she took the time to hang it with care. Her fingers ran over it and she knew she would never look at it or wear it again without thinking of Marc. She smiled at the sentiment. Who was she kidding? There was no one wine, no one outfit, no breeze, no song, no food that would serve to bring Marc to her mind. He would be there always and in her heart.

Chapter Sixteen

The next morning, the light streaming into the room was Libby's first awareness. The second was the sound of a knocking at the door.

She slipped out of bed and wrapped herself in a bathrobe. The thick carpet felt soft underfoot as she trod to the door and peeked out the viewing hole.

"Marc."

"I woke you. I am sorry." Marc handed her a cup of coffee as soon as she opened the door.

She adjusted her nightgown, covering as much of herself as the slip of material allowed, as she sank onto a chair. Automatically, her hand smoothed her hair. Only after her first sip of the strong drink did she ask, "What time is it?"

"It is only nine. Would you like to go back to sleep?"

"Nine!" She sat up. "I never sleep this late."

"You are on the holiday."

"Do you have work tomorrow?" she asked with a wild hope that he didn't and that this idyllic time didn't need to end right away.

"I will go to work when we get back."

Now Libby felt guilty. Here she was, virtually on a summer-long holiday, and he had to go to back to work immediately, and after the night they'd had. She shouldn't have slept in so long either.

"Well then," she said, sighing dramatically, gazing at the lofty ceiling, the carved woodwork, the silk drapery, "we have to hit the road."

"Breakfast first."

"Give me five minutes."

When they reached the restaurant, Marc chose a table in the square. As she settled in, Libby admired the arena across the way. It looked smaller from outside, but the two tiers of arched openings were amazingly intact even though the structure was thousands of years old.

"Are any of those walls original to the building?" Libby laid her napkin across her lap and sipped appreciatively at the coffee the waiter placed in front of her unbidden.

"All of them, I think."

"It's so old."

"If I remember my history lessons, it was started in the first century and expanded in the third."

"Imagine that."

"Marcello! *Ciao. Come stai?*"

Marc half rose to greet the handsomely dressed couple

when they reached their table. A short burst of Italian went over Libby's head, then she recognized Marc's Italian words as he introduced her.

"Mi permetta di presentar la al mio amico Libby Zufferlia. Libby, these are old friends of my family, Milo and Bette Corneo."

She smiled, offering her hand. *"E un piacere."*

Without being asked, Milo held the back of a chair as Bette slid into it. She too put the napkin across her lap and settled in for a chat. Libby shook her head slightly, telling Marc not to worry about the interruption when she caught his apologetic smile.

Striving to be inclusive, Bette used well-schooled English. "But where is Anna?" Bette asked. Without waiting for his reply, "Did she look lovely?" She turned to Libby. "I saw her shopping for the dress."

Libby's confusion must have been clear on her face, "The dress?"

"For the opera." Bette asked Marc, "Where were you sitting? I looked for you so we could all go out for a drink."

"Bette—" He switched to Italian.

Bette and Marc talked animatedly, hands gesturing the whole while. Libby only caught a few words but the way Marc's face paled told her there was a story she needed to hear. The sympathetic smile Milo offered her while the other two carried on their discussion had Libby's heart sinking.

These people had expected to see Marc's mother this morning, she had recently purchased a new dress, and

Libby knew Anna Iacome was celebrating a birthday very soon—in a matter of days, wasn't it? She raised her fingers to her lips to mask her dismay. You didn't have to be Nancy Drew to read the clues. Anna Iacome assumed that she was going to the opera with her son as a birthday gift.

At Milo's prompting, Marc and Bette ended their conversation abruptly. Libby eyed Marc speculatively. He frowned. And suddenly dissatisfied with his chair, he shifted several times in his seat while his hand rubbed his midsection. An upset stomach? She had seen that movement before.

She addressed the table as her breakfast was set in front of her, "Please, feel free to speak Italian. *Scusa. Non parlo italiano.*"

They paused for a half a moment and then Bette asked Libby, "Zufferlia. Do you have the family here?"

Marc jerked. Libby watched him as she answered, "My grandmother was brought up in Croce. I have cousins, aunts, uncles . . ." Her voice trailed off.

"Zufferlia," Bette said again in a musing tone.

She asked Marc something. He looked embarrassed and was about to answer when Libby realized what was going on. These people were from the Croce area. They had probably chosen sides in the Loszach versus Iacome feud.

"Loszach," Libby said in a tone louder than she intended. "My grandmother is—was Mattia Loszach."

Bette's eyes widened. She gave a tense smile but her eyes darted toward Marc. Then, without even looking at

Libby, she launched into a full-fledged saga about something. Milo chuckled at his wife's anecdote while Marc smiled pleasantly. Libby could tell Marc was mortified and doing his best to cover it.

Good. Be mortified, Libby thought as she pushed her food around on her plate. How could he allow them to be rude to her like that, just because she was a Loszach? In the village it was one thing. She pulled herself up short. Why? Why was it one thing in the village? She nibbled at her eggs enough to give the semblance of calm. Remain calm. It was her mantra. Remain calm.

The men argued good-naturedly about paying the check, Marc won and settled the bill. Farewells were made with polite words to Libby, and the two couples separated.

Walking side by side although not touching, Libby and Marc made their way to the car in silence. It was going to be a long drive home.

Chapter Seventeen

Some distance from Verona, Libby broached the subject first. "So, Marc. What's the deal? Do you always take your mother to the opera for her birthday?" Remembering her mantra, remain calm, she kept her voice low and even.

"No. I don't always take her." His tone was argumentative.

"Marc, are we splitting hairs here? Tell me."

Marc glanced quickly from the road to Libby. "Splitting hairs? What?" His exasperation sung out. "Speak English, please."

Libby remained silent, waiting until he spoke.

"Okay, yes, I have taken my *madre* to the opera a couple of times, but I didn't ask her this time."

"Oh, Marc. She probably saw the brochure on your hall table the night I went to dinner at your house. I did."

"I didn't have the time to hide it," he said defensively. "She didn't tell me she was coming."

"Oh, I feel terrible. She's probably very hurt."

"Yes, I know that!" he snapped.

"Why didn't tell me you took her every year? As much as I wanted to go on the trip, I would have understood."

"I've taken her three times. Not every year."

"The last three years in a row?"

He lifted his shoulders. "I bought her an even better gift."

Libby looked out the passenger side window at the stream of trucks they zipped past. How could a caring man like Marc be so thoughtless of his mother's feelings? Of her feelings? Her fingers rubbed away the lines forming on her forehead. She has been so flattered by his generosity. His thoughtfulness. She had enjoyed thinking the trip had been a plan of his making, with her and only her in mind. It was all clear now. He had booked them for his mother and himself.

He pressed the flat of his hand against the horn and swerved into a tiny gap between two trucks. Libby braced her hand on the dash. "She went shopping and bought a dress."

That, to her, was the saddest part. That his mother poked around shops with the night at the opera in mind, a night when she would have her son all to herself. Libby remembered shopping, moving hanger after hanger, trusting she would know the right outfit when she saw it. Trying clothes on until she felt she looked just right. Choosing her the two-piece black silk with care. Then she remembered Vivia's warning about Libby taking care of her heart.

"I bought her a tree. She will like that very much," Marc all but barked.

She'd never heard him sound so cross before. Perhaps she didn't know the man at all. They were arguing about his mother, but that wasn't the crux of the disagreement. It was the way he had allowed her to be dismissed by his friends at the restaurant.

She must disengage from this argument. What was the point, after all? He didn't love her. He didn't even respect her, if his feelings for her extended family were taken into account. She was trapped in the car with him, still an hour from home. She took a calming breath. She needed distance. She needed her nonna.

She tried to convince herself that the timing of this argument was ideal. She'd get her nonna settled and, in a few days, fly back home. Wash her hands of the whole stupid Iacome-Loszach feud. She risked a glance at his handsome profile. A muscle twitched in his jaw. She bit hard on her bottom lip to keep the tears in check.

When they reached Croce, Marc pulled his car over to the curb next to the alley leading down the mountain, to her house. He opened his door to get out.

"I can take it from here, Marc." She reached over the seat for her bag. "I enjoyed last night. Thank you very much for a wonderful time." Her voice sounded hollow.

"Libby—I'm angry at myself . . ."

"I understand, Marc. Go make peace with your mother."

She swung the garment bag over her shoulder and with a lightheartedness she didn't feel, she put a bounce in her step. She knew he would watch her until she was out of sight. Jaunty. *That's me.*

Once she turned the corner, she allowed her shoulders to droop. She felt wretched. How could twenty-four hours be such a roller coaster of emotions?

She prayed that Nonna was there in the house—she desperately needed her comfort—but on the other hand she didn't want her to see her in this state. Libby paused and ran her fingers under her eyes. Amazingly, her face wasn't wet with tears. She pinched at her cheeks to give them some color, took a few shuddering deep breaths, and straightened her shoulders once again.

As she neared the house, she found that she didn't have to mask her feelings. The air outside the door smelled of Nonna's cinnamon rolls. Libby's mouth watered. She was genuinely anxious to see her grandmother. A smile lit her face.

"Nonna?" She pushed open the unlatched door.

"There you are, honey. I was hoping you'd walk through the door any minute. I'll put the kettle on, but first come here and give your old grandmother a hug."

Libby melted into the embrace, feeling the love, acceptance, and security it represented. Her grandmother patted her back with the familiar, there-there movement that made Libby happy to feel like a child in her presence.

"Oh, Nonna."

"Yes, we have much to talk about, don't we, child?"

It was Libby who filled the kettle as Mattia lifted the pan of baking from the oven and by the time the tea was steeped, Mattia had drizzled a thin swirl of icing over each roll. Napkins, mugs, and plates sat in front of the women on the scarred old table as they eased onto the kitchen chairs. Without formality, they dug in.

Libby licked her fingers shamelessly. "Oh, Nonna, that was a terrible scene at the flea market."

"I should have warned everyone that I was coming. But I . . . well, I wanted to see how Leo really felt without giving him time . . ."

"What happened between you and Leopoldo Iacome, Nonna?"

Mattia patted her hand. "All in good time. You go first, dear. I know you went to Verona. That much Vivia told me when I picked up the key. But it was what she didn't say that told me that you went with Marcello Iacome. Even as a girl, that Vivia enjoyed a mysterious air."

There had never been need to equivocate with her grandmother. The truth was best. She took a deep breath and was surprised at its jagged sound.

"Nonna, I love him. I have fallen head over heels in love with Marc. When I first saw him, he was so handsome and seemed interesting. I thought we'd have some fun together this summer. But I fell in love. I didn't mean to but there it is."

Mattia opened her mouth to speak but Libby rushed on, hoping to deflect any criticism. "If you knew him, you would understand. He is kind and gentle. He's funny and caring. He's thoughtful—well, I thought he was thoughtful but . . . what's the point?" She bent her head and cupping her face, she spoke into her hands. "It'll never work out and now I will just head home and go back to my life."

Mattia touched her granddaughter's shoulder. "What has happened, Libby? He is thoughtful but he is not thoughtful. What happened?"

Resting her chin in her palm, Libby abbreviated the tale of the evening before. She told of the magic, the romance, and then the abrupt return from cloud nine to earth as the couple joined them at brunch.

"His poor mother thought she was attending the opera with him. She bought a dress—and she bragged about her generous son too, no doubt, otherwise how would these people know?" Libby paused to take a breath and then, shaking her head at the memory, rushed on once more. "And Nonna, he was so thick-skinned about it. Kind of cold, you know? It was a side of him I had never seen before. And that's not the worst of it—well, maybe the worst of it as far as his mother is concerned, but not for me. He . . . he . . ."

"Calm down, sweetie."

"He tried to hide the fact that I am a Loszach!"

Mattia smiled and then frowned. "You are a Loszach! That you should say that. How this village seeps into one's blood. They have you thinking that way." She clicked her tongue and shook her head. "But you said he tried to hide that fact?"

Libby explained the exchange at the table that morning. "And Marc just let them look at me that way!" She took a breath. "It sounds so stupid when I say it out loud."

"No, my dear, I know exactly what you mean. I am very sorry that you were dragged into this mess. I wouldn't have asked you to come if I'd had any idea."

"Oh, I know that, Nonna."

"Well, honey, no doubt there was a lot going on with your young man, things you can't understand. Have you met his mother?"

"Oh, yes. She is a piece of work." Libby held her head imperiously and assumed an accent, making her grandmother laugh. "She's all, 'I am Iacome.' She looks down her nose at me. I had never actually seen anyone do that. I thought it was just an expression. But no."

Tipping her head back, Libby tried to re-create the expression Anna had used with her outside of Marc's house, but managed only to cross her eyes. Her amusement was brief as she added sadly, "And now she is hurt and she will never like me."

Mattia smiled gently. "But, Libby, I don't understand. If you are going to go home anyway . . . and if she was so unfriendly with you, then why does it matter so much to you?"

"I don't know, Nonna. I don't know. She is his mother and she thinks badly of me. And Marc was dishonest . . ." She wrapped both hands around her mug of tea and shook her head, sighing.

Reaching for the teapot to refill their cups, Nonna said, "Well, let me tell you a story of dishonesty."

Mattia's eyes took on that far-off look one gets when remembering the long past. She told a sad tale of a young woman—a girl, really—who was in love. A girl whose family disapproved of the love. Of a young man whose family also disagreed with the proposed marriage. And of a time when the village was their whole world, where, isolated, the people had to reconcile the new boundaries the world imposed and the mistrust that grew from them. Each member of their families was on the other side of that trust. Of soldiers and broken hearts.

In Mattia's recounting, Libby remembered how she and Marc had sat at this table on the night of the storm, struggling to understand bits of their families' history. What had been only an abstract story then now took on deeper meaning. Libby could picture Mattia as a young woman and Leopoldo, a young man. In her imagination, she saw herself and Marc. Betrayal and lost love.

"Did you keep your love secret, Nonna?" She was thinking of the way that Marc had insisted they keep their relationship secret.

"For a long time, yes. Then we decided we would wed."

Croce, 1948

Mattia thought she was going to faint, really faint. Her knees shook so badly that she pressed the Bible down on them hard. The priest had finished the mass and was crossing to his podium to make the community announcements. Mattia heard a scuffling sound from across the aisle, from where she knew Leo sat. She looked back and saw him rising. She licked her dry lips and stood as well.

"Mattia?" her mother hissed.

Mattia ignored her. She stepped fully into the aisle and, still facing the altar, felt Leo take her hand. She looked into his face. He was pale and nervous-looking but he squeezed her fingers and gave her a brave smile. They strode to the front. All around them voices buzzed.

"Father," Leo said loudly, "we wish to announce our betrothal."

The priest frowned down at them. "Betrothal?"

"We wish to marry."

The buzzing rose in volume. Mattia could hear her own parents' voices and a girl's that was probably that of Deborah; she'd always had a crush on Leo.

"No!" Mattia's father was shoving past his wife in their pew. "No!"

"This is a house of God!" the priest called. "Sit down."

Mattia didn't dare look around at her father. The humiliation at being talked to that way would make him furious.

Deborah's voice rang out. "May I speak, Father?"

The priest looked around but everyone had quieted and were watching Deborah who had stood. Still, he gave them all a stern warning look before saying, "What is it, child?"

"I think it's my duty to say, to tell you about her, about Mattia Loszach."

Mattia felt alarmed and confused. She looked to Leo but he shrugged. He didn't know what she meant either.

"One of your parishioners was colluding with the enemy during the war and Mattia knew about it." Once again, voices rose but the priest warned them into silence. "Her friend, Sophia, used to meet with him in the woods."

"No, that was—"

"Let her have her say!" the priest barked.

"And she's the reason that Giuseppe got shot."

"No!" Mattia felt aghast that Deborah could stoop so low.

"I saw Mattia and Sophia with them in June. I heard them talking."

"That had nothing to do with—"

"You were with American soldiers?" the priest asked.

"This has nothing to do with Leo and me," she cried.

"Sophia is pregnant with the enemy's baby right now!" Deborah crowed.

Now those assembled were standing and looking for Sophia. The poor girl had her face buried in her mother's lap.

"Stand up," the priest ordered.

"Leave her alone!" Mattia cried. She dropped Leo's hand and tried to go to her friend but suddenly she was surrounded by people. Her father and uncle lifted her body and carried her out of the church.

Croce, present day

Libby realized that she had been pressing her hands against her mouth in horror. She dropped them. "Oh, Nonna, how awful."

"It gets worse, child." Mattia took a sip of her luke-warm tea. "My father had been talking about moving to Canada for a while by then. That's one of the reasons that Leo and I decided to make our announcement in church that day. But as soon as we got back to the house, my father ordered my mother to start packing."

Libby reached for her grandmother's hands; they felt cold and clammy.

"I was locked in my room but I heard the commotion in the middle of the night. The crying. The wailing. It seemed to be everywhere, outside, inside . . ." She paused and looked around. "In this very room. They told me later that they dragged Sophia out of the church and . . . and . . . tormented her."

"Oh, Nonna."

"That night, my best friend Sophia disappeared."

For a horrified moment, the only sound was the tick-ing of the clock. Libby felt the tears rolling unchecked down her face. "Was she found?"

"Eventually. She'd run off with the soldier." Mattia smiled softly. "You can hardly blame her."

"But Leo must have known the truth, about you hear-ing about the soldier long after the war. It's not your fault his brother was killed." It never occurred to Libby that her grandmother did anything wrong.

"Libby, Sophia was pregnant. To be pregnant out of wedlock, that was a terrible scandal, and then to have the father be American! You must remember that when I was a girl, the Americans were our enemy."

"But what she said about her causing Leo's brother's death?"

Mattia stood and moved around the kitchen, from the door to the sink to the window. "Not true, of course. We were just children in the war. It was years later that Sophia met that man. But you see, Leo still mourned his brother, missed him every day. When I didn't deny that I knew what Sophia was doing, he just believed Deborah. He believed that my friend collaborated with the enemy."

"In the heat of the moment, perhaps."

"In a way, I blamed him for Sophia's situation, her leaving her family that way."

"You did?"

"I was so hurt and mixed up. Just a girl, really. And Leo was just a boy."

"Well," Libby said, feeling defensive, "he's had a lot of years to figure out the truth."

"Yes, it was a malicious tale borne out of jealousy by Deborah. She wanted Leo for herself and knew it would take very little for my father to emigrate. In my heart I blamed him. I went with my family willingly to make a new life in Canada. And the saddest part is, he never knew what Deborah really was, what she had done, and he married her."

"He should have at least written to you."

"I married Geno so quickly, you see . . ."

Libby easily pictured it: Leo's anger, then later his calm, his reflection. Probably by the time he realized that Sophia's soldier came long after the end of the war, Mattia and her family had already left. And they went so quickly, they wouldn't have left a forwarding address. By the time he'd heard news of Mattia she was probably married. No wonder he was so angry.

Libby met her grandmother at the window. "Marc once told me that Deborah thought she had a loveless marriage and she blamed you."

Mattia's eyebrows lifted. "Really?" Then her expression sobered. "I'm sorry for that. Deborah and I never got along."

"What about Nonno? Did you love my grandfather?"

"*Cara,* my dear, yes I loved him. He was a fine man, a good husband, and a wonderful father. And you remember"—she touched Libby's nose with her fingertip—"he was a loving grandfather to you and Anthony."

"But?" Libby prompted.

"But Leopoldo. He was my first love and, I am sorry to say, Libby, if it causes you pain, he was my great love. I believe, if we are blessed, each of us has one great love. He was mine."

Libby put her arms around her grandmother. They stood woman to woman, no generations divided them.

Mattia reached for the tissues, straightened her shoulders, and forced cheerfulness into her voice. "You know, I rushed into this old house, full of memories, knowing that until I saw you nothing could soothe me except to bake."

They laughed. It was typical of Nonna and the reason the cupboards were stocked. No matter the problem, baking was her escape. "I haven't really even looked at what you've done." Holding out her hand to take Libby's, she added, "Give me a tour."

With great pride, Libby led the way to the sitting room. Glancing around, she noted that Enzo had been here. His tools, though always stored in an orderly and tidy manner, were now gone. There was no sign of construction now. *Perfetto*, Libby thought, pleased at the timing.

Tugging on Mattia's hand, Libby urged her grandmother on. "Don't stop here. I've got to show you my crowning glory." She led her through the sitting room straight to the small, efficient washroom. Both stood inside the room as Libby regaled her grandmother with this glorious feat. They chuckled as Libby relived each plumbing nightmare until victory was hers. "This tiny room is the greatest of them all."

Mattia paused once more in the sitting room, nodding with approval. "I will be very comfortable here, Libby. It is bright and cozy." She took her place on the sofa and surveyed her surroundings. "And the sun pours down through the open staircase. This is a very clever design. You are a very clever girl."

Libby snuggled against her grandmother, drinking in the praise. "I'll show you your room in a moment."

Mattia patted Libby's thigh. "We are quite the pair, aren't we? These Iacome men somehow get into our blood."

The women remained silent for a long while. Sitting close together, they each allowed the other time to digest what had happened in the last forty-eight hours since Nonna's sudden appearance on the day of the flea market. There were so many questions. So many answers. But there was time.

Libby glanced at her grandmother. Her eyes were closed and her body relaxed. Perhaps she'd sleep for a while. Vigorous though Mattia was, Libby still worried that she pushed herself too hard. She looked toward the staircase, wondering if she could steal upstairs and get a blanket without disturbing her. Instead, she remained where she was, taking a moment to admire the room. She seemed to be on the go so much these days that she had yet to really appreciate the full effect of the changes she had overseen. And helped to make. She had been no slouch with the tools and had worked side by side with Enzo for many days.

Pleasure overtook her. The sun from the window above did do so much to brighten this room. And even the shadows the sun cast as it moved in and out of the clouds added another dimension. Libby was too tired to think about Marc, although the ache was near the surface.

Shadows danced on the sitting room wall and along the staircase. She knew the house well enough now that she was able to distinguish the source of each from the floor above. The latch on the second floor window cast a silhouette reminiscent of a little mouse on the wall. The tiny dappling above and below the shadow mouse was caused by the imperfections in age-old glass. Shots of rainbows dancing here and there were from the leaded bevel on the perimeter of the panes. All of these she knew instinctively. She frowned in concentration as her attention was drawn to a mystery shadow, one low on the wall, almost at the floor, thin and straight as an arrow. Libby used her memory of the staircase, each stair, the upstairs window frame, and the edge of Nonna's bedroom door to determine the source of this peculiar shadow. Nothing matched. She gave up trying to guess its origin and angled her head. Still no answer from this vantage point.

Her grandmother stirred briefly as Libby slipped away from her. She moved toward the stairs and the shadow.

An unease settled on Libby before she could have ever formed the thought. Crouching slightly she made her way deliberately to the shadow. She hunkered down and turned her attention up the short flight of steps. Waving her hand slowly, she determined the angle of the sun as her hand blocked the light. Her eyes followed, slowly, examining.

She stood and moved to the fourth step from the floor. There, wedged tightly against the wood on either end, was a narrow strip of wood about an inch from the stair tread. The length of a dowel. Her hand hovered above it, unwilling to touch it. Could someone have left it there accidently? Slowly she put out her index finger and flicked her nail against it. It was strong and tight. It was virtually invisible against the wood of the stair treads.

Libby's eyes flew to her sleeping grandmother. Her heart pounded. Someone did this on purpose. Someone hoped that the wood would make a person descending the steps fumble, trip, and fall. And Nonna had been there alone. Someone wanted to hurt Nonna.

Chapter Eighteen

Fury settled cold and hard in the pit of Libby's stomach. Someone dared to put Nonna at risk! Someone dared trespass on her home. Someone dared. What kind of person would do that? The very thought of leaving her grandmother there in the village without exposing the culprit was inconceivable.

Libby placed a toss cushion on the step, in case her grandmother woke. She didn't want to move the stick until she'd shown a few people. Then she began toward the kitchen, toward her bag, toward her telephone.

"*Permesso?* Do I smell the baking in here?" Vivia's gentle laughter filled the room. She stood at the doorway as was customary. She wouldn't enter without invitation, unlike whoever jammed the dowel on the stairs.

Libby moved toward her cousin. She felt furious.

241

"Libby? What has happened?" Vivia rushed to her side.

"Someone was here. Someone tried to hurt Nonna."

Vivia hurried to the sitting room door. Seeing Mattia as Libby had left her, snoring softly, blissfully unaware on the sofa, Vivia swung back to her cousin's side, confusion clearly imprinted on her face. "You must explain to me. I am not understanding you. Mattia—she sleeps, Libby. She is not hurt."

Libby led her cousin to the stairwell. She removed the small pillow and pointed, directing the other woman to the fourth step.

"Look," she whispered. "There."

Leaning in, Vivia stared intently, angling her head this way and that as if trying to figure out why someone would brace a length of wood in such a dangerous place. "I understand." Vivia leaned against the wall beside Libby.

Mattia slept.

"We have to find out who did this."

Wordlessly, the cousins moved together to the kitchen, each to their bags for their phones. Vivia took hers just outside the door into the courtyard and flipped it open. Libby mirrored the action from the kitchen.

"Enzo. Yes, it's Libby. I need you to come up to the house. Yes, now!" Her fingers pressed a button to end the call and then punched in another. "Marc. Someone has come uninvited into Nonna's house and . . . and left something. I need you."

Clicking the tiny instrument closed, she sank into the

chair and waited. Her pulse beat on, loudly, making Vivia's Italian seem a fast hum in the distance.

"How long did I sleep?" Mattia, appearing in the doorway, stretched her arms out and up, smiling in a sheepish way.

Pandemonium ensued as the house began to fill. The first on the scene were Melena and her three children—Carmela, fresh and sweet as a toddler should be, Lisa, pretty, shy, and quiet, choosing to stay behind her mother, and Mico, unreadable, sullen, and distant. Close behind them came Drago, out of breath, untying his apron. He had run down the hill from the Loszach Bakery apparently.

The grapevine was in full force that day because hot on Drago's heels came Uncle Victor, his wife, Natale, even Great-Aunt Erika bustled into the room. They met one another with kisses and as the Italian flew, each explained the story to the other, pointing to the evidence on the stair. Mattia joined in, her shoulders moving in the decidedly Italian way. With each intonation of a question, answers came louder, anger or disbelief underlying all.

Libby stood stock-still, amazed at the unity presented by these people. Family. Mattia's family. Her family. Drago's voice rang out over the others with a single word that created a sudden hush: "Iacome." And as quickly as the hush had fallen, up rose a flurry of angry words, each speaking louder than the last.

Libby slid out of the room and out of the house. She breathed in the early evening air and the silence the small court offered. She looked around at the beauty of this little hideaway. She had always meant to bring it back to life. To show the gorgeous stone work under the growth. To put furniture out here. Automatically, she bent and began yanking weeds from between the stones of the terrace.

Iacome, she mused. She understood why her family would think of them. She herself thought of no other. Perhaps whoever came in had been invited? Had a key? The evidence pointed to sweet, kind Enzo. She knew he'd been there because his tools had been removed. This couldn't be. Enzo? Quiet, dear Enzo.

Then again, just because she couldn't comprehend this deep-seated loathing these families shared, it didn't mean it didn't exist. It could have been Enzo.

At precisely that moment, Enzo and Marc appeared from the path. They hurried to her side, Enzo speaking in his special brand of rushed Italian and broken English, while Marc stood silently, studying her face closely. Her heart skipped a beat at the sight of him.

Libby faced Enzo squarely, removing his hand from her arm. She ignored the concern his face carried and addressed him directly. "Enzo, you were here in this house. While I was in Verona, while Mattia was in Udine, you came here." She deliberately framed it as a statement.

Enzo nodded vigorously, even before she had finished speaking. "Yes. I was here. I clean. I pack my tools. I have it ready for you. For Mattia Loszach." He waved his arm, a gesture meaning the entire house. His eyes shone with pride. "No more work. I have it ready for you to live."

Libby studied his frank expression. His generous admission of his work and his intent. She said nothing.

Marc spoke first in Italian to Enzo and then to her. "What is this about, Libby? What has happened? Is your grandmother all right?" He laid a gentle hand on her arm as his eyes swept over her.

Libby stepped back from both Iacome men and answered evenly. "Yes, she is fine. But she might not have been. Someone came into this house and set a trap for her. On her new staircase."

After a flurried exchange, both men headed inside. Libby followed, calling to them. She hadn't told them the room was full. Of the Loszach family. Through the kitchen, toward the sitting room, Marc went with Enzo close behind.

Drago blocked their entrance.

Before a word could be spoken, a pounding could be heard on the front door. Silence fell. Libby took a halted step forward. No one ever used the front door. People always let themselves in the side gate and came to the kitchen. Unless they were Iacome men, Libby thought. They came up the hill secretly and stole through the small courtyard, unseen.

Mattia was first to the door and swung it open. There, handsome and strong, was Leopoldo Iacome with Anna and Marc's aunt Marana flanking him. His deep baritone rang out in English, "What is this story that people tell?"

He reached for Mattia as if by instinct, but caught himself before his hand touched her. Seeing she was fine, his glance took in all who stood behind her. Mattia stepped back, offering the three Iacomes admittance.

Marc and Enzo moved through the throng toward their family members and Drago stepped in front of Mattia with the balance of the Loszachs taking a place behind him.

"This is a Loszach house. We will not have Iacomes as our guests."

Marc swung around to face Drago. "Do not address my family that way. They came here out of concern."

The two men squared off, eyes trained on each other, shoulders and feet moving slowly.

Libby couldn't take one more minute of this. "Out!" she demanded, arm outstretched, finger pointing at the door. "Out! Take this out of our house—both of you! Go!"

Marc and Drago froze, staring at her, uncomprehending. Libby stepped forward and spoke to both men through gritted teeth. "I am sick to death of this feud. This stupid vendetta. I will not have it."

Murmurs circulated the room as one person would translate for another. She turned away and marched to the staircase, up onto the second step. She raised her voice and addressed the group from above them. "Here is what this Iacome-Loszach feud has got us." Her finger pointed to the all but invisible dowel on the step.

The fury had returned. It replaced all sadness. It replaced all weariness. She had nothing to lose. She had no place here. "Who did that? And why? Because of being from the mountain or the town? Where people, where their ancestors, came from? Because someone is from the Loszach family and someone is from the Iacome family? Is this reason to come in to this house uninvited and try to hurt someone?"

She could see Enzo shaking his head. Confusion was evident as the translations ran around the room. They looked from Enzo to Libby.

Libby went on, bitterness ringing in her voice. "Here's a shocker, everyone! I hired Enzo to do this work." She waved her arm as she spoke, indicating the fine state of the house. "He came here—an Iacome came here—every day. And worked. And a Loszach paid him. Imagine that! Nice job too, wouldn't you say?" She paused dramatically, sarcasm lacing her tone, her words. "Most of you have already said it is an excellent renovation."

Libby lowered her voice a degree. "The most shocking thing in all of this is that you'd be the most upset by hearing that two members of your rival families actually worked together. You're not shocked that Drago and Marcello would want to fight."

Marc spoke out then, cajoling, "Libby."

Libby met his glance and said directly, "You and I have other things to discuss in private."

Heads on both sides of the families swiveled between Marc and Libby at the statement. Murmurs rose again.

Libby pressed on. "That's shocking too, isn't it? That Marc and I would have something—anything—to say to each other." Her laugh was a biting one. "More shocking even than the fact that Mattia could have been hurt today. And all of you—you accept this. You think that one family has a right to hurt another." Her voice broke as she whispered, "What is the matter with you people?"

The murmuring grew louder as Enzo pushed forward. He pointed at the wood. "I did not." His hand covered his heart.

Libby could see the earnestness on his face. "Well, someone did this. Someone came in here. Sneaking around like a nasty, mean-spirited child to play a dirty little dangerous prank."

Suddenly, she knew. Her heart stopped beating—just for a moment. She knew.

There wasn't a sound in the room. For its great number of people there wasn't a sound. All eyes were on Libby. Her eyes scoured the room. Searching.

There, in the corner, standing slightly behind his mother was Mico. As their eyes met, Libby knew she was right. It was a dangerous, childish prank. A prank that could have been costly.

Melena straightened under the scrutiny. Confused by the sudden attention, she followed Libby's gaze. Turning to see who was behind her, Melena gasped. Mico Loszach had begun to cry.

Water sprayed over Libby's head. She turned to direct the shower to her shoulders where tension had created hard knots. As it beat and soothed her skin, she closed her eyes to the memory.

Now alone in her shower, Libby allowed the tears to

flow. For Marc and what she'd lost in him. For herself and the lonely life ahead. Scrubbing the tears away with the heel of her hand, she told herself, enough. She was a realist. There were no fairy-tale endings. Or fairy-tale middles for that matter. Life was life. You lived it. You managed your expectations and then disappointment wouldn't be as bitter. Oh, Libby, who are you trying to kid?

She twisted off the flow of hot water and gasped as the cold spray shocked her body. There. Enough is enough. With an extra vigor, she rubbed her skin dry, leaving it pink after the minor assault. She needed to feel something besides this hollow longing. This void where her heart had been.

After the startling revelation that exposed Mico, mayhem had taken over. A confusion of Italian reigned while Libby stayed put, but felt removed emotionally.

Melena and Drago were appalled. Mico had some notion that if he scared Mattia Loszach she would go home with her granddaughter and his father could have the house. A house to rent to tourists. Just like his father had discussed. He didn't think that a fall could really hurt her or maybe even kill her. He and his sisters fell down all the time. He didn't know. Drago and Melena led Mico home to deal with his behavior in private.

The rest of the Loszachs headed for the kitchen. Good Italians that they were, they prepared coffee and laid waste to Nonna's cinnamon rolls. A dinner in Mattia's honor was planned for the following night at Uncle Victor's. Uncle Gerardo and Celia would be called.

Libby shook her head, smiling at the memory. Yes, as true as morning following night, no matter the circumstance, the Italians shared a meal.

From the step, Libby had seen Mattia speak with the Iacome family as they prepared to leave. As she opened the door to the street, she and Leo stilled, looking into each other's eyes. Leo's eyebrows lowered, but not in anger so much as in confusion.

Anna Iacome had watched the elderly couple, her expression unreadable. As though feeling Libby's gaze, Anna turned and met her eyes. Libby saw clearly a small smile form around Marc's mother's lips, as her head gave an almost-imperceptible nod in Libby's direction. But as to its meaning, Libby remained unsure. Victory, no doubt. Anna laid her hand against Marc's arm as he held the door for his mother and aunt to step outside before him. He didn't look back.

Now, Libby slathered lotion over her body. Well, she'd done it, she'd burned her bridges behind her. She had called Marc out in front of his family. In front of hers. Embarrassed him. Exposed his duplicity. Accused his family of trying to hurt Mattia. He was obviously furious.

Libby shrugged into her robe and eased her wet hair away from its collar. Because her grandmother was asleep on the second floor, she headed up the dark exterior stairs to her room. Tomorrow evening she'd join the rest of the family at Uncle Victor's dinner, and tell them then that she was going home. Immediately.

She tugged on her closet door and looked for a cozy

nightgown. She found the soft sweatshirt she had worn the day of her hike, the day Marc joined her on the mountain. Her eyes filled with tears. As she reached in to pull out her slippers, her hand brushed against the parcel Enzo had given her at the flea market. She had forgotten it entirely.

She carried the hefty little bundle to the bed to sit while she opened it. Her fingers held a small envelope she hadn't noticed before. She slid it open and read the tiny card. *With love.* But no signature.

She closed her eyes to remember the day at the flea market. It was a mere three days ago but seemed like a lifetime. In her mind's eye, she could see Marc standing in the sunshine smiling at her. He had motioned with his head and wagged his eyebrows playfully for her see Enzo. But she had been preoccupied by Anna, by his mother's proximity. And by his clandestine hand-holding, brief though it had been. Libby remembered trying to maintain an air of friendly ease. Now she saw it clearly, that smile, making his beautiful eyes crinkle, so mischievous.

Curious now, she tore at the plain brown paper. In her hand, she held an antique door knocker. Beautiful and ornate. Oh, the irony. From a man whose whole relationship with her had to be secret. A man who stole up to her balcony under the cover of darkness. And left the same way. A man who wouldn't dare to be seen with her in public. He—of all people—would give her an ornament for a door that he would never use. Tears scalded her face. She held it to her breast, to her heart.

Chapter Nineteen

Libby blinked repeatedly. The morning sunlight was bright and strong on her face. She eased herself into a sitting position and glanced around her room. Memories of yesterday flooded her mind. What a dreadful day.

She crossed the room to the old dressing table and grimaced at herself in the mirror when she caught sight of the state of her hair. With a few no-nonsense brushes, she contained it, and then with deft fingers, worked it into a French braid. Tidy and out of the way.

Coffee first, she ordered herself, as she slid into her jeans and tank top. She slipped downstairs, expecting to find her grandmother, but the first floor was unoccupied. As she filled a mug with the coffee that stood waiting, and scrounged around for something to eat, she heard her grandmother's footsteps above. But she didn't make her presence known. She still felt too raw to talk.

Blowing and sipping on her coffee, Libby trod back to the third floor. She leaned against her bedroom's door frame, forming a plan of attack. She would have to make calls and book a flight of course, and then . . . this room. Packing and clearing away all evidence that she had ever been there. It was hard to believe. She had been happy here since May. Well, she reminded herself, until recently.

She was leaving Italia. Her stomach jumped at the thought.

Libby lifted her chin. It was for the best. She had become an emotional wreck in this past week. She had shed enough tears to last her a decade or so. With quick, determined movements, she grabbed the bedclothes and began to snap them into shape. There, in the rumpled bedspread, was the door knocker. Paper and all. She had slept with it, like an old familiar teddy bear. She lifted it and held it. Marc had given her a gift for the front door, a gift that he himself would never use.

At the mere thought of Marc, tears threatened once again. *Oh, no. I can't begin this again. I will not allow it.* It was sad. That much was true. To love and to lose. Songs, poems, books had been written on the subject. But she and Marc knew from the get-go that they shouldn't be together. Couldn't be together. Their families, the wretched feud . . .

And then something clicked. In her brain. Not in her heart this time. She stood stock-still and tossed the gift onto her bed. Tossed it away like the meaningless bauble it was.

Think, don't feel, she berated herself. *Think*. Why was she crying? How did this happen? How did she reach the point where she stood there wallowing in self-pity?

Suddenly it dawned on her.

Marc could use the door of this house anytime he wanted. It was not at her request that their friendship, their love, remain hidden. He could have made their relationship known. He could have celebrated their time together. The truth, as it often did, tasted bitter.

Marc Iacome chose not to.

He could choose to do anything he wanted and yet, he chose to keep their relationship a secret.

And she had permitted it.

She stepped out onto her balcony in the morning's soft yellow light. Drawing a flattened hand up to shield her eyes, she looked down the grade of hillside to the Iacome vineyards.

"Okay," Libby told herself, aloud, "so he's at work presumably." She moved to her closet and grabbed her sneakers, and slipped her bare feet into them. Her purse. Her car keys.

When she reached the second-floor door, she stuck her head inside and yelled to her grandmother. "I am going to the winery. I have some unfinished business there."

Marc Iacome had had enough drama to last him a lifetime. As he moved from vine to vine, he stewed. He had wanted to slam the Loszach front door behind him yesterday, but his upbringing prevented it. Instead he had meekly clicked it shut and made his way with his family toward the village car park. His grandfather and Enzo had walked ahead. He knew his cousin inside out. He knew Enzo's good heart and his honest nature. And Marc also knew that Enzo had been deeply wounded by Libby's unfounded accusation. That Enzo would ever hurt a fly was more than Marc or any Iacome could credit. Where did Libby get such an idea and what would possess her to say it?

In another part of his busy head, he couldn't help remembering how she looked, standing above the group. Her color brightened, her eyes flashing, her body, so tall, lean, and imposing. So angry. So commanding. Libby Zufferlia looked as beautiful as any woman he had ever seen.

He shook the image aside and reminded himself that he was angry. She was not the only person who could be angry.

Yes, she had crossed a line. She had told him to get out. Imagine. Get out. She had telephoned him, after all! She had said, "I need you."

Damn that Drago Loszach and his big feeling ways. It was his fault that she told them both to get out. And if that weren't bad enough, she turned on him again and all but told him, Marcello Iacome, to shut up. But the material point was she accused Enzo, the poor guy. Publicly.

And Drago Loszach. Who did he think he was? If he hadn't blocked Marc's and Enzo's way, then Libby wouldn't have gotten so angry and then none of this would have happened.

As it was, he had already been in very hot water with his mother yesterday about the whole opera thing.

Women! There was no winning with them.

Marc gave his midsection a rub. It couldn't be hunger. It was still early and he had eaten breakfast. It tasted like sawdust, but he had eaten it.

He whipped his hand tool from his back pocket and used his pruners with perhaps a little more force than necessary to remove extra leaves from the grapevines. The fruit should have as much of this sun as possible.

He paused to look up and down the aisle of vines. Not another soul within sight. Good! His people knew when to clear out and give a man some room. A little space. Some sunlight. The earth under his feet.

He glanced at his watch. Only a few minutes had gone by. He breathed in the clear air, still cool before the day's heat, and concentrated on work, on the vines. A little rain couldn't hurt. Not too much though.

Again, Marc rubbed his hand against his solar plexus. He was just like his grapes, his vineyard. He needed to find balance.

"I got the door knocker." Libby knew her voice startled Marc from his work on the grapes. "Until last night I thought the gift was from Enzo—I had set it aside given everything that happened after the flea market. I just opened it last evening."

She had stopped at the end of the row of vines, close enough to see him clearly but far enough to remain distant. Physically and emotionally distant. She was patently aware that she was on his turf. Literally.

Marc's eyes narrowed and his expression was wary. He didn't respond.

"An interesting choice of gift."

Marc remained silent. Watching.

"I am dying to know what you were thinking when you bought it. I'd love an explanation." Her voice was calm, but sarcastic. She took a step forward.

Marc cleared his throat and asked, "What do you mean? It was a fine piece. Excellent craftsmanship. It was a housewarming gift. I saw it, I thought of you and your house and . . ." He lifted his shoulders.

"For a door you would never use—not a Loszach front door! And you didn't give it to me, anyway. Did you? You passed it to Enzo. Like a schoolboy passes on a note so his buddy can give it to the girl—in grade three, perhaps." She was warming to the topic now.

"Libby, I was with my mother. You know how it goes."

"Yes, I see very clearly now how it goes. I see how you work."

His confusion was evident and he opened his mouth to interrupt. She forestalled by raising her index finger.

"Let me tell you what I see when I look at you. I see a man who is a leader in his community. A grown man who has now taken the reins of a large and prosperous family business—an empire some might say." She drew her gaze from his face to sweep over the orderly, flourishing vineyard and the stately buildings in the distance.

"And this same successful businessman hides behind his mother's skirts."

Marc's face darkened with anger. It didn't intimidate her. Instead she strained to ignore the shape of his face, his eyes, his mouth, and how they filled her with yearning.

She paced side to side in the narrow row. "From the very first moment I met you, you used the women in your family shamelessly. They could be your excuse for treating me, our friendship, our relationship, as nothing more than a secret tryst to be concealed. They wouldn't approve, you said. Oh, you dressed it up in pretty little Romeo and Juliet analogies, but the truth is you never wanted me. You never wanted me to be yours, truly yours."

Marc took a dangerous step toward her and instinctively she stepped back. Her heart hammered in her chest. She knew, as it knocked there behind her rib cage, that it was breaking.

Breaking.

She pressed on, rallying her courage against tears. "The plan you made—to have Enzo and I meet about the house renovations, to meet in secret, you kept it up. You would come to me, stealing through the night, like a man shamed, to my balcony. And you left the same way. Always sure that no one would see Marcello Iacome was having a relationship with a Loszach. In order to be with me during the day, we left the village. The mountaintop, Venice, even Verona!"

He had moved closer now. "You wait one moment."

Libby held up her hand to silence him. "I am not without blame. I am heartily ashamed of myself. I permitted it. Perhaps in some way, encouraged it. In my own defense, I tried to tell you how I was feeling. But you kept on about the feud—our families—until I believed it. I believed you."

"That's enough. You know the difficulties surrounding our family history."

"Oh, yes, Marc, I know. You tell me often enough. The feud is between you and Drago—the two swaggering heads of the families. You two keep it going, this medieval vendetta. Never approach a Loszach, never hire a Loszach, never speak to one with any civility. You, who others look to for leadership. For guidance. For what is acceptable behavior. You have prolonged and fueled this bad blood between our families."

"That is not true! I am an Iacome and have known since I was a child of the long list of grievances your family has committed against mine. The Loszachs have caused my family pain. Even your own grandmother . . ."

"Not my grandmother, Marc. Yours. Speak to Leo about Deborah."

Though tears pushed from behind her eyes, she straightened her shoulders and forced strength back into her voice. "I love you, Marc, but I will not fan this flame any longer. I will not do any more to perpetuate this myth of a feud."

Marc looked around, seeming desperate to understand.

Suddenly Libby felt drained. "For my part, Marcello, it is over."

He narrowed his eyes. "There. You've had your say. Now it is my turn." His voice brimmed with bitterness. "Since I met you, all you talked about was your life back home, about leaving." He swung around, frustrated, and faced down the long alley of trellises. "Until now, you never told me that you loved me. I don't understand you. What do you want from me, Libby?"

Libby sighed a ragged, deep sigh and turned to go. "I guess I just wanted to dance with you at the bonfire. In front of our families. To show our love. To feel no shame. I just wanted you to accept me. To feel proud of what we had. To love me as much as I loved you. That's what I wanted. I am leaving, Marc. Leaving Italia. Good-bye."

She turned away abruptly and, head down, watching her feet, she hurried over the rich earth, along the row of vines.

Libby had moved through the rest of the day, trusting herself to dress and respond automatically. She accepted the dull throbbing, the ache that had taken her over. It would be with her a long, long time. But for this evening, she was determined to absorb as many memories of her family as possible. Large, rowdy, noisy, and loving.

Uncle Victor's house was full to capacity and overflowed into his yard where tables had been set up under the stars. The breeze rustled in the shrubs around the garden's perimeter. Lanterns rocked gently from the boughs of olive trees. Above them, Montagna Croce loomed forebodingly, a black silhouette against a shimmering navy sky.

Libby raised her glass now in a toast Victor made in honor of Mattia's return. It was good to know that this group, this family, would be close to Mattia, keeping her safe and happy. She looked over at her grandmother sitting there serenely. Only someone who knew her inside and out, as Libby did, could see the melancholy behind the smile, the determination in the shoulders.

At that very moment, Mico approached Mattia. She turned her full attention on him as he, glancing to his mother for support, began, "I am sorry, Mattia Loszach. I did not mean to kill you."

After a murmur of translation, the adults all laughed. Mico looked discomfited but only for a moment. Mattia took his hands in hers and said gently, "Mico, here is my forgiveness. You take it." She opened one of his palms and placed an imaginary item in it. "It is yours. It is for you to keep until someone asks for your forgiveness and then you too must give it quickly and willingly." She embraced the boy and then, seeing the embarrassment so typical of boys his age, released him.

From her chair, Libby watched Melena and Drago share a smile, pleased to have the episode laid to rest. Beyond the long tables, Drago paced, looking from his watch to Mattia and then to his watch again. It was a curious behavior that no one else seemed to notice. All were engrossed in predinner conversation, laughing and sipping wine.

It was Drago, moving quickly toward the garden gate that had Libby craning to see who else could possibly be joining them. All family members were present and accounted for.

A hush fell over the group as Drago stepped to the foot of the table, near the garden wall, clinked his glass with a spoon and asked for everyone's attention.

Mystified, Libby was even more surprised that he addressed them all in English and then in Italian.

"My family, tonight we celebrate forgiveness. Forgiveness between Mattia Loszach and my little foolish boy." He looked pointedly at his son, who smiled so trustingly at his father. "And now I ask for forgiveness from Marcello Iacome."

Libby's heart skipped a beat. Suddenly dizzy, she squeezed hard on the arms of her wooden chair.

"And I in turn ask for forgiveness from Drago Loszach." Marc stepped through the gate from the darkness of the village into the pool of light.

Libby gaped, stunned, until a cry of joy from her grandmother had her realizing that Marc wasn't alone. Leo Iacome was flanked by Marc's mother on one side and Enzo on the other.

"*Cara,*" Leo cried. "Will you forgive me?"

"Leo, oh . . ." They met in a tight embrace.

Marc held out his hand to Drago. "On behalf of the entire Iacome family, I ask that we now lay aside our differences and begin a new tradition of friendship."

Drago clasped Marc's hand. After a shocked silence, the whole gathering stood and clapped.

Libby smiled broadly through her tears as Marc moved to her side. Her heart had begun to hum. With hope.

He cupped her face with his hands and wiped her tears away with his thumbs. She leaned into him and he kissed her forehead.

Marc turned to their family members and spoke clearly, though his voice was thick with emotion. "I must now ask Libby for her forgiveness. Until today I did not know I was a man of such foolish pride. I hurt this beautiful, brave woman. And I am sorry."

As he drew her a few feet aside into shadows of the garden, a hush that had fallen on the gathering did nothing to give them the privacy they wanted.

Facing Libby he said solemnly, "Do you forgive me?"

Libby didn't try to stop the tears, though this time they were of pure joy. "I do."

"Do you still love me?"

Nodding, her voice breathless, she said, "I do."

Smiling now, Marc Iacome asked, "Do you promise to marry me?"

Stepping into his waiting embrace, Libby responded with certainty, "I do."

Marc shot his cousin a meaningful glance and, reacting to his cue, Enzo's deep baritone rang out, drawing all attention to him. Soon, Drago responded in the tradition of the Alpine singing. Back and forth the melody went in a chorus that spoke of love and commitment. For the first time in generations, all male voices from both Iacomes and Loszachs were raised in harmony instead of response and retort.

There, before their families, Marc and Libby danced.